BROTHER *FROM A* BOX

Also by Evan Kuhlman

. . . .

The Last Invisible Boy

EVAN KUHLMAN

BROTHER FROM A BOX

ILLUSTRATED BY IACOPO BRUNO

Atheneum Books for Young Readers
New York London Toronto Sydney New Delhi

ATHENEUM BOOKS FOR YOUNG READERS
An imprint of Simon & Schuster Children's Publishing Division
1230 Avenue of the Americas, New York, New York 10020

ATHENEUM BOOKS FOR YOUNG READERS
is a registered trademark of Simon & Schuster, Inc.
For information about special discounts for bulk purchases, please contact Simon & Schuster Special Sales at 1-866-506-1949 or business@simonandschuster.com.
The Simon & Schuster Speakers Bureau can bring authors to your live event. For more information or to book an event, contact the Simon & Schuster Speakers Bureau at 1-866-248-3049 or visit our website at www.simonspeakers.com.
The text for this book is set in ITC New Baskerville.
The illustrations for this book are rendered in pen and ink.
Manufactured in the United States of America
0312 FFG
First Edition
2 4 6 8 10 9 7 5 3 1
Library of Congress Cataloging-in-Publication Data
Kuhlman, Evan.
Brother from a box / Evan Kuhlman ; illustrated by Iacopo Bruno.
p. cm.
Summary: Sixth-grader Matt Rambeau finds out what it is like to have a brother when his father, a computer genius, creates a robot kid that goes to school with Matt, shares his feelings and ideas, plays, does chores, fights for his "life" when chased by spies, and becomes a part of the family.
ISBN 978-1-4424-2658-0 (hardcover)
ISBN 978-1-4424-2660-3 (eBook)
[1. Brothers—Fiction. 2. Family life—New York (State)—New York—Fiction. 3. Robots—Fiction. 4. Artificial intelligence—Fiction. 5. Schools—Fiction. 6. Adventure and adventurers—Fiction. 7. New York (N.Y.)—Fiction.] I. Bruno, Iacopo, ill. II. Title.
PZ7.K9490113Br 2012 · [Fic]—dc23 · 2011033973

TO THE THREE MBs,
WITH GRATITUDE AND
APPRECIATION

1.

I have a new brother.

His name is Norman.

He arrived six weeks ago in a big wooden box.

And that was when the trouble began.

2.

The trouble began when I pried open the box, wondering what was inside.

And before I knew it, I had a kid pestering me. But he wasn't *really* a kid.

And before I knew it, I had a brother, but he wasn't like anyone else's brother, anywhere on earth.

And before I knew it, my family and I were kind of famous, but none of us wanted to be famous.

All because of Norman.

Some days, I tell you, I wondered if I could ditch the kid.

You know, like take him to the comic book shop on 81st Street, then run away really fast. But I'm sure he would have found his way home. Norman has an excellent GPS system.

Or maybe I could ship him back to France, when Mom and Dad weren't paying attention. But I probably couldn't afford the postage, so . . .

Hey, anyone want to buy a kid? He comes with his own box. Make me an offer. Cash? Video games? Your dog? I'm listening.

5.

The day that Norman arrived started out pretty normal. I woke up, went to school, tried to learn some stuff. But when I got home, it turned freaky on me.

Having survived *yet another* scary encounter with Big Vic's crazed beagle from two buildings over—the dumb dog thinks he's a pit bull—I had just stepped off the elevator, hungry for a snack and what Mom calls my "daily fix" of kid TV, when I saw Leon, the building super, standing next to a big crate and pounding on the door to my apartment.

"Hello in there?" he said loudly. "I am *not* lugging this box up here a second time. . . . Hello? . . . Anyone?"

Leon finally saw me. "There you are," he said, blowing out air. "Package delivery."

I had pretty much figured that out on my own. I found my keys, opened the door, and looked at the box. It was nearly as tall as I was and appeared to be very heavy. I was hoping it was a gift for me but figured it was something Mom or Dad had ordered for the apartment—

furniture or an appliance. "Can you bring it inside?" I asked the super.

Leon wiggled his mouth into a frown. "Didn't I tell you about my recent back surgery?" he asked, rubbing his spine and wincing, then sticking out a hand. "A gratuity is pretty much standard in these kinds of circumstances."

I fished through my pockets, but found only my MetroCard, fifteen cents, and a stick of gum. "Can you hit my dad up next time you see him?" I asked.

Leon snarled up his face, then lumbered toward the service elevator. That man just never looks happy. Poor guy.

I pulled the keys from the door lock, sized up the crate, then wrapped my arms around it and started dragging it inside the apartment, pretending I had muscles the size of watermelons and tugging a big box would be no sweat. But man, was it heavy! What the heck was inside it, a car engine?

A bronze statue of someone famous?

A baby elephant?

Probably not a baby elephant.

When the box and I were inside, I dragged it a few more feet into the living room, jostled it, and pushed it lengthwise onto the rug, hoping I didn't break something when it hit the floor with a *thump*.

"*Aïe!*"

That was weird. It sounded like the box said, "Aie!"

Like a person sound. But since shipping people in a crate was probably against the law, I decided that the sound must have been my imagination, which my mom and dad say is "overactive." Trust me, it's the only part of me that is overactive.

Oh. Later I learned that *aïe* is French for "ouch." But as far as this story goes, it's not yet later.

I circled the box, wondering what those foreignish words stamped onto the wood were saying to me, then stooped and read the address label. Whatever was inside had been shipped by international express delivery from the Institut d'Intelligence Artificielle in Paris, France, to Matthew Rambeau PhD, 555 West 83rd Street, Apt. 10C, New York, New York, 10024 USA.

That's right, I live in Manhattan, but please don't think of me as a snooty rich kid. For one, I don't have a snooty bone in my body. Also, I never have much cash, as the building super can attest to. But my dad is a college professor and my mom is a social worker, so we're not loaded, but we're not going hungry, either.

Where was I. . . .

Oh. The Matthew named on the address label is my dad, not me. We have the same name, but Dad gets to add some letters due to his going to college and getting a doctorate degree in computer science.

Bummer for me. I had been building up fresh hope that whatever was inside the box was a late-arriving birthday present from one of my relatives in France, where Dad is from, and where his name is spelled Mathieu and is pronounced like you are sneezing halfway through it—Ma-*tewww*. A new bike or even a snowmobile would have been cool, but instead it was probably computer parts for my dad, a devoted computer nerd. Mom sometimes says that we own enough motherboards, monitors, and memory modules to build a first-rate missile defense system.

Since the box wasn't for me, I headed for the kitchen to make a grilled cheese sandwich, but stopped in my tracks when I distinctly heard something inside the box say, *"Bonjour?"* And then the box became interesting again, because this time I didn't think it was my overactive imagination. I know that *bonjour* is a French word that means "hello." My imagination imagines in English.

And then something inside the box said, *"Hola?"*

And then something inside the box said, *"Namaste?"*

And then something inside the box said, *"Salut?"*

And then something inside the box said, *"Goedendag?"*

And then something inside the box said, *"Jambo?"*

And then something inside the box said, "Hello?"

"Hello," I said to whatever was inside the box, quickly wondering if I was having some kind of brain flip-out that sometimes happens to kids under too much stress, hearing voices coming from inside a box and then talking back to the box. Next stop, the Home for Brain-Frazzled Kids, Manhattan branch.

"Ah, you speak *anglais*, English," whatever was inside the box said, kind of muffled. "Fortunately, English is one of the forty-six languages included in my language oscillator. *Comment allez-vous?* How are you?"

"I'm fine, how are you?" I said. Part of me was wondering why I was being so polite. Another part was wondering what the thing inside the crate would say next. And the largest part was thinking, *There's a living kid stuck inside a box without any airholes.*

I must rescue him before he suffocates!

I ran into the kitchen and hunted through the tool drawer for something I could use to pry open the box. While I was doing this, the thing inside the box said, "*Ça va bien, merci.* I'm fine, thank you." And then, "*Bonjour?*"

"I'll be right there," I yelled, thinking that what was happening was not even in the same galaxy as normal. Something living, something *human*, was trapped inside that box, sent all the way from France. And I was talking to it and planning its rescue.

Grabbing a hammer, I hurried back to the box and used the claw part to pop off several tacks, and then I started prying at the planks. That seemed to take forever, and was interrupted by the thing inside the box asking what I was doing, and me explaining what I was doing. And yes, I was very aware of how bizarre this all was. It almost felt like I was living some other kid's life, while in an alternate universe the real me was munching on a grilled cheese sandwich and watching cartoons. It was messing with my brain.

At last I tossed two big planks aside, then tore through a mound of straw and packing peanuts until I reached a full-sized boy wrapped in bubble wrap, except for part of his face.

Freaky to the moon and back! I mean, how would you react, finding a living kid in a shipping crate? I swear I saw stars, and maybe even a few planets, but I did not pass out. But I'm not saying I didn't come close.

"Are you okay?" I said to the boy. "Can you breathe in there?"

As the kid said something in French I didn't understand, I unwrapped some of the bubble wrap and saw— *oh . . . my . . . godmothers!*—that the boy in the box looked sort of like me. Similar face, but his hair was lighter and longer, and his eyes were bluer and his nose was a tad nosier, and . . . hmm, something wasn't right about his skin. It was too perfect. Too pink and smooth. Me, I have a small scar above my left eye from the day I wiped out while riding bikes with my parents in Central Park: I was trying to avoid running over a humongous dog turd that should NOT have been on the pathway. I veered left, hit a rock, and went tumbling. It hurts just thinking about it.

Anyway, the kid in the box didn't have a single scar or mark. Not a freckle or a speckle, not a dent or a ding. I almost wanted to scratch him, just so he wouldn't look so perfect.

His clothes were pretty normal, though—a red-and-white-striped pullover, jeans, socks, and sneakers—except for a black beret that no kid in America would be caught dead wearing. No jacket, so he must have been cold, traveling to New York from France, I thought. But maybe the straw, packing peanuts, and bubble wrap kept him warm.

While I peered at the boy in the box, wondering why he was shipped to us from France, and how long he was planning to stay, and if his family missed him yet, and if he was hungry and thirsty, and how he was able to keep from going to the bathroom while in the crate, and also if he liked grilled cheese sandwiches, the kid's eyes suddenly grew large and he blinked several times, and I heard what sounded like the whir of a fan or a small motor kicking in.

"Mon dieu, mon enfant!" the kid said. "My God, child. Where is your box?"

4.

I did a bunch of high-quality thinking, trying to come up with an answer to the question, *"Where is your box?"* I figured that this kid with the beret, having spent a few days in a wooden box, and going without food or water, might believe that all kids lived in boxes, making me the boxless freak while he was the normal kid.

"I don't live in a box," I said, "but it looks really cool and fun."

No, I didn't really believe that living in a box was cool and fun, but I was being nice to a person from a different culture. Mom says it's important to be nice to everyone, not just people who look like us and talk like us and smell like us. I think she's right, except when it comes to girls. Being nice to girls goes against everything I stand for.

So I said to the kid, "Would you like to come out of your box? Are you hungry? I can fix a snack—do you like grilled cheese sandwiches? Grape juice? We also have milk, but milk snots me up. Does milk snot you up?"

No answer from the boy, who was still giving me that creepy *Where is your box?* look. His head was tilted at a weird angle, and he was scanning me up and down and side to side, like I was a book he was reading. Then it dawned on me that he must be totally stiff and achy after being stuck in a box for who knows how long. He needed my help!

I reached in to yank him out, putting my hands under his Frenchy armpits, and pulled kind of hard, and I came away with the *top half* of a boy, his hips and legs and feet left behind in the box.

Ackkkkkkkkkkkkkkkkkkkkkkkk!

I just killed the boy in the box!

Ackkkkkkkkkkkkkkkkkkkkkkk!

I couldn't think. I needed to think. *Ackkkkkkkkkkkkkkkkkkkkkk!* I just killed him! *Ackkkkkkkkkkkkkkkkkkkkkkkkk!*

Just as I was about to go call 911, my brain kicked in, and I noticed that the kid didn't look close to dead, and there was no blood or guts anywhere. And then I saw cables sticking out of where his belly ended, the kind you use to hook up game machines and DVD players to a TV.

A kid with cables? Maybe on Planet Weird! I held him as far away from me as I could. What I *really* wanted to do was throw him as far away as I could, and hide in my closet until Mom and Dad came home. They'd know what to do. They *always* know what to do.

But I didn't want to hurt the poor kid. A near-hysterical giggle bubbled out of my chest—hurt him? I had just torn him in half! At the giggle, the boy smiled at me like he didn't know that I had left the lower half of him in the crate. I had seen worms survive when chopped in two, but never a kid.

And that could mean only one thing. The kid was—drumroll, please—a fake. A machine! A robot! Cool, cool, cool. Even though Norman wasn't sent to me as a birthday gift, I was highly jazzed. We owned a talking robot! Could be lots of fun. Way better than a new bike or a snowmobile.

I sat the top half of Norman on the rug and quickly pulled the rest of his pieces out of the box—hips and legs covered by jeans and feet covered by socks and shoes—and lined them up in the proper order. Everything smelled new: new jeans, new socks, new shoes, new kid.

Meanwhile, Norman was giving me a funny look.

"*Êtes-vous bien?*" he asked. "Are you okay?"

I realized that I probably looked as pale and weird as I felt. So I slapped my face to move some blood there, smiled like everything was shipshape, and looked around to make sure this wasn't a crazy dream. But everything looked too normal and boring to be part of a dream. Everything except the broken-in-six robot kid from France.

"I'm fine," I said. "But what about you? You're in pieces!"

"*Oui,*" said Norman. "And eager to be assembled, *s'il vous plaît.*"

I gazed at the top half of the boy, and at the body parts I had just pulled out of the box. "You're a robot, right?" I asked.

The kid flickered his eyes like he was searching his brain. Later I learned that Norman has no brain, just an advanced Axiom 96 quad-core central processor in his head, and lots of microprocessors and sensors throughout his body. But it's still not later.

"*Non,* not a robot," he said.

"An android?"

"*Non,* not an android."

"A cyborg?"

"*Non,* not a cyborg."

I couldn't think of anything else he might be.

"*Excusez-moi,*" the boy said. "Ask me if I'm an artificial, genetically enhanced, cybernetically integrated, bionically modified life-form."

O-kayyy. "Are you an artificial, genetic . . . whatever you just said?"

"*Oui!*" he said, smiling weirdly, the left side of his smile going way up and the right side hardly moving. "Model number NRM 2000-B at your service."

"Cool," I said. "So, um, hi, model number NR—uh, what did you say?"

"Model number NRM 2000-B at your service," he repeated.

"That's a mouthful!" I said. "Can I call you something else? How about . . ." I searched my brain, and the only name that popped out was this one: "Norman? I'm Matt, by the way."

"Nice to meet you, Matt," the machine said. "*Mon frère.*"

As has already been proven, I'm not the smartest kid in the world, but I do know that *mon frère* means "my brother." My *brother*? The crazy robot must have wonky programming, I thought. "Garbage in, garbage out," my dad likes to say.

Wonky programming or not, I realized that Norman could be a cool toy, once I got him snapped together. Maybe I could even train him to fetch comic books or my iPod. And fix sandwiches for me while I'm watching TV! Oh! Oh-oh-oh! And do my homework—at least math problems that normally give my brain trouble! And a thousand other things!

I always thought it would be fun to be so rich that I had my own butler. I guess a robot butler named Norman would have to do.

5.

I found Norman's assembly instructions packed in the box, but they were written in French. I hardly knew any of the words, except the ones that looked like English words such as *attention*, which in France is probably pronounced in a funny way: *a-ten-shee-own*.

And I finally got why my mom was on me to take French this year at school. I protested, saying that there were probably twenty people who spoke French in all of New York. Spanish was the way to go, and why not wait until next year when my brain would be that much bigger? Boy, was she going to give me the big I Told You So when she met Norman. Knowing more French would have come in mighty handy.

I stared at the directions, as if staring at the funny-looking words would cause them to decipher themselves. And then I realized that Norman spoke English and French. He could translate. I held the instructions up to his face.

"Can you read this for me?" I said to him.

"*Oui!*" the robot said. "*Félicitations pour l'arrivée de votre nouveau . . .*"

"No! I meant please read the instructions in English," I said.

Norman blinked his eyes, wiggled his mouth, rolled his shoulders, and then read the instructions in English. The first step was to hook up the cables dangling out his belly to cables inside his hips, then to "unify" the top half of his body with his hips, and fortunately there were diagrams on the other side of the instruction sheet to show how to do that.

Even though I was feeling weird about it, I followed the directions and connected the cables, then twisted the hips into the top half of Norman and locked them in place. Easy as pie, and Norman didn't seem to mind. In fact, he sang a song while I was working about a *"petit prince"* living in a *"grand château."* *Petit prince* meant a small prince, and I thought that a *château* was a house. Small prince, big house. I wasn't sure that was something worth singing about, but hey, what do I know?

"You now have hips," I told the robot.

"Excellent!" he said, smiling, but he also looked a little nervous. I suppose I'd be nervous too if I was being snapped together by a twelve-year-old kid who can't tell a pair of pliers from a wrench. Might end up with a backward foot. Every time Norman tried to walk, he'd do the splits.

The next instructions were less freaky, but still freaky in their own way. I had to twist and lock his legs into his hip sockets, and then twist and lock his feet into his legs, Norman watching me while I worked.

The thing was together now, a complete fake kid, but he stayed sitting on the rug.

"Do you know how to walk?" I asked.

Norman shrugged, which caused a creaking sound. I wondered where Dad kept the WD-40 or the bike chain oil. I had no idea, really.

So I jumped up and helped Norman stand—he's a few inches shorter than I am. The robot seemed to be testing his feet, rolling them, to see if they would hold him upright.

"Are you ready to strut your stuff?" I said.

"Comment?" Norman said, but I was pretty sure he heard me and understood what I said. He was stalling, I figured, asking questions as a way of avoiding doing something he didn't want to do. I've used that tactic. It buys me time, but eventually I end up doing the thing I was trying to avoid.

We might as well get this over with, I thought. "Walk!" I ordered the robot.

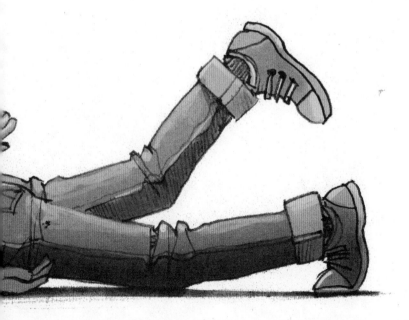

"Oui." Norman looked over at his shipping crate like he'd rather be inside it than outside, grabbed my left hand, and took a shaky step forward with his right foot, and then a shaky step forward with his left foot.

"C'est bien?" he asked, his voice modulator raising his voice up a notch, not quite girly but getting there. "How am I doing?"

"Not too bad," I said. "But try it without my help."

I let go of Norman's hand. He took a step, teetered, and fell on his face. *Splat!*

"Aie!" the robot called out, kicking his legs like he was trying to get to his feet that way.

Hilarious! No way was kicking his feet going to make him stand up. That won't work, dummy! I almost busted some gut tubes, I was laughing so hard.

So I'm not a perfect kid. Get over it.

6.

I helped Norman until he was able to walk on his own.

"Pardonne-moi," Norman said, while I was demonstrating my own walking skills, marching across the living room and back again. "How is it that you are able to walk so gallantly?"

"Years of practice?" I said, shrugging.

And then I thought about those scenes in movies and TV shows where the mom and dad get all mushy while watching their baby take her first steps, and I wondered why I wasn't getting mushy watching Norman take his first steps, especially now that he was doing better.

Were my mushed-out genes damaged? I wondered, a little worried that they might be. I'm not the most emotional kid on the planet, don't usually cry during sad movies, and junk like that. Still, I will say I felt a pinch of pride when Norman walked all the way across the room without tripping or holding on to anything along the way for the first time. Though, I thought I heard a fan kick in inside his stomach, like his hard drive was straining and needed cooling down. Robot stress, I guessed.

"Good job," I told him. "You're a natural!"

"*Merci*, Matt," Norman said, crawling inside his wooden box and arranging himself among the packing peanuts and straw. *"C'est beaucoup mieux."*

"Uh . . . I don't follow. Can you translate?" I asked.

"Those words mean this is much better, being back in my box," he said, smiling in the weird, uneven way.

Norman gave a little shimmy, causing peanuts to settle around his neck, and I thought I understood why the robot wanted to be inside his box. It did look cozy, with the straw and peanuts, plus there were no dangers inside that crate. No terrorists or muggers or bullies, or psycho beagles named Meatzilla (!!!) snapping at your legs when all you want to do is go home. Just Norman, foam peanuts, and straw. I sort of wanted my own box to crawl into.

I was also getting crazy hungry for a snack, and thought again about fixing grilled cheese sandwiches for Norman and me. And then my brain switched to a different thought, and I wondered what a robot kid was even doing here. Could Mom and Dad be considering replacing me with a well-behaved robot that always remembers to make his bed and clean up after himself?

Before I could get a serious freak-out going, Norman

suddenly slumped and went dead. Didn't blink. Didn't move a muscle. No fan or hard-drive noises.

"Norman?" No answer. "Norman!" Still no answer.

Great, I fried Norman, I thought. Did I hook up his cables wrong? Or burn him out due to stress from having to walk too soon after being put together? Just as I was starting to feel bad, I remembered: He's just a robot, a machine. Maybe we could ship him back to France for repairs, or order a different model.

I hate it when new toys break on the first day.

7.

Coco le perroquet aime manger des craquelin. I just remembered that sentence from a picture book, written in French, that my dad used to read to me when I was a little kid. The words mean that Coco the parrot likes eating biscuits.

Though I'm not exactly sure how useful this information will be. Never mind!

8.

Norman wasn't fried. What a relief.

Amid all the stuff that came out of the box when I pulled Norman out was what looked like a laptop charger, only bigger. A light flicked on in my head. Norman probably just had a dead battery! (Later I learned that Norman is powered by four sixteen-cell lithium ion battery packs. But it's still not later yet.) So I inspected him, searching for a place to plug in the charger, and found a port in his left armpit.

Feeling kinda oogled out by what I was about to do, I carefully plugged one end of the charger into Norman, and the other end into a wall socket. Norman didn't move, and his eyes were closed, but underneath his eyelids I could see a small green light slowly blinking, which must have meant that his batteries were taking in juice.

Norman lives!

Dad came home while Norman was charging.

"I see that the NRM 2000-B has arrived," he said,

dropping a stack of student papers onto a table. My dad teaches computer science classes at New York University, and sometimes fixes their busted computers just for fun. "He's a few days ahead of schedule, but that's okay. Adaptability is a hallmark of the evolutionary process, right, sport?"

Okay, so it was Dad who ordered the robot from France. That made perfect sense. Probably every computer nerd dreams of owning a PC that can walk and talk and play a decent game of chess. Me, I'm more of a checkers kind of kid.

"Have you and André had a chance to get to know each other?" Dad asked, stretching his arms and cracking his knuckles.

André? I told him that since the robot didn't come with a name tag, I had named him Norman. Dad shrugged and said he was planning to name him André, but since I "beat him to the punch," Norman would do just fine.

While my dad circled Norman's box, I told him that I had put Norman together and taught him how to walk, and now I was charging him because his battery went dead.

"We'll have to fix that," Dad said. "André, I mean Norman, should not lose power without advance warning, and not until after using up the reserve battery. Probably just a loose wire somewhere. But nice work on the assembly, junior."

"Thanks," I said, almost blushing. I love it when I do stuff right.

Dad roughed up my hair, then kneeled near Norman's crate. "Amazing," he said, running two fingers along Norman's face, which would have given me the giggles, but the robot stayed in recharge mode. "I've seen photos, videos, and 3-D models, but in person André—Norman!—looks so much more lifelike. So much more . . . human."

"Almost too human," I said, wondering how long it would take for the robot to charge. "I've never seen a kid with hair and skin that perfect."

"Good point," Dad said. "Norman may indeed appear too perfect to pass for human. I hadn't considered that! Though an intentional downgrade would raise ethical issues, including but not limited to whether Norman should have a say in the matter, or is it okay for us to act on what we perceive to be his behalf without his prior consent?"

I got confused halfway through that sentence.

While a bunch of questions were bouncing around inside my head, like did Mom know about his latest gadget, Dad told me how Norman came to exist. The robot was created by my dad and his brother, Jean-Pierre, who is also my uncle Jean-Pierre, who is also a scientist at the Artificial Intelligence Institute in Paris, France. My uncle designed the hardware, and my dad wrote the software, and then Jean-Pierre's girlfriend,

Véronique, and two assistants built Norman and one other prototype.

"What's a prototype?" I asked, feeling like I was spending too much time on the dumb side of the street.

"A prototype is the first of its kind, a test model," Dad said. "There are inevitably going to be some bugs to work out before you release it to the general public."

"Norman's smile is weird," I told him, trying to screw up my smile as a demonstration.

"I can fix that," Dad said, winking, which is always strange because my dad doesn't wink right. He holds the wink too long, and just when you think his eye is stuck shut, it pops open. My dad might be the only adult in the whole world who doesn't know how to wink.

As I was about to ask Dad why he and my uncle decided to build robots, and how come kid robots instead of adult ones, we heard a whirring sound. Norman opened his eyes, saw Dad, and cried out, *"Papa!"* Papa? Huh? And then the robot launched himself at Dad in a way no real kid could, like a rocket booster kicked in. Dad fell back onto the rug as Norman kissed his cheek like a zillion times.

I think they do a lot of that in France, people kissing each other even if they aren't in love. It's probably a cool thing in France, but over here it looked kind of dumb, probably because Norman is a robot, and robots, at least the ones in movies, aren't normally big kissers.

Might go on killing rampages, but you never see them kissing people.

And it looked like Norman was going to kiss Dad to death, for cripes' sake! Dad was putting up with it, which I also didn't like. I mean, this was *my* dad, not Norman's. Get your own dad, crazy robot!

Eventually, Dad pushed Norman away, saying, "I like you, too, but that should do it for now." He sat up and placed Norman on the rug, but the thing scooched closer to Dad like he'd be miserable if he had to be more than three inches from *my* father.

Grrr.

"Uh—Dad? Why did Norman call you 'papa' and me 'brother'?" I asked.

Dad drew an arm across his face, even though it looked like it was free of robot spit. "Norman is programmed to recognize you as his brother, me as his father, and your mother as his mother. Several image and video files of us are stored in his CPU."

"Oui, c'est vrai," Norman said, smiling. "Accessing relevant JPEG and MPEG files immediately." He blinked, and his left hand twitched. Dad would fix the twitching hand thing later. But it's still not later.

While I was wondering why the robot was programmed to recognize us as his family—since, being people, we are not his family—I heard someone coming up the hallway outside our apartment, and the familiar sound of Mom jiggling her keys into the lock.

Dad's face nearly dropped to the floor. "Here's the thing," he said to me. "Your mother does not know about Norman—I thought I had another day or two to break the news to her. So . . ." He had a wild look on his face, then said something utterly absurd: "Let's hide the robot and deny everything!"

Let's hide the robot and deny everything—that's something I'd say! But since we had only a few seconds, and were panicking, I helped him hide the robot, though we did a lousy job. Dad dropped Norman in his box and we smoothed packing peanuts and straw over him, then Dad and I stood in front of the box like two murderers trying to hide a body from the police.

We are so busted, I thought, as the door opened with a ghostly creak. *Eeeeeeeeee . . .*

9.

My mom's name is Connie Rambeau, but before she married my dad her name was Connie Weston. She's thirty-seven, one year younger than Dad, and she works as a counselor at the Community Help Center in Brooklyn. When people run out of money, or lose their job or their house, or don't have electricity because it was shut off by the power company, they go to my mom and she tries to find money for them, or a job, or a place to stay, or whatever they need. It's a really important job.

I'm telling you this stuff so you know that my mom is normally a good person. Try to remember that, because she might not sound too cool or too good for a while yet.

Anyway, Mom stepped inside the apartment, set her portfolio on a table, and smiled at Dad and me. "Mommy is home, as may be evident by the fact that I'm standing here," she said. My parents talk funny sometimes. It must be a smart-person thing.

Normally Dad would give Mom a big kiss and ask how her day was, and I'd go give her a hug and listen to how her day was. But Dad and I stayed standing in front of the shipping crate like two goofs. It was beyond dumb, since we weren't wide enough to hide the entire box. It stuck out on both sides of us.

"Welcome home, honey," Dad said, clearing his throat.

"Hi, Mom," I said, feeling my legs wobble.

Mom gave us a curious look and came closer, her eyes moving to the crate. "Was a package just delivered?"

"Nope, no packages were delivered," my dad said in a jumpy voice. "Right, sport?"

Thanks a big bunch, Dad! I froze, since there was nothing good for me to say. If I said there weren't any packages delivered, then I'd be a liar. If I told the truth, Dad could get in trouble. So I pretended that my mouth wasn't working. Wanted to talk but couldn't.

Mom rolled her eyes, then aimed an arm at the crate. "What is that, a hallucination? Is there or is there not a big wooden box on the floor?"

"Oh, *that* wooden box," Dad said, tugging at his blue tie, the one with the tiny dolphins on it. "Just some LCD monitors and motherboards."

"Monitors? From France?" Mom said, looking like she wasn't interested in buying the pound of baloney Dad was trying to sell her. "It says the box was shipped from France. It's right there on the wood!"

"Sure, they're starting to make outstanding monitors

in France," Dad said, pinching up his face. That was probably another lie. The French are too busy kissing each other to make great monitors.

Mom peered at Dad, and at me, and at the box, and then she frowned and took a step toward the kitchen. But just as I was thinking we'd gotten away with hiding Norman, I heard a weird *th-th-th-th-th* sound, like the robot was snickering underneath the straw and packing peanuts.

"Did you hear that?" Mom said, no longer aiming herself toward the kitchen.

"I didn't hear anything," Dad said. "Did you hear anything, junior?"

Thanks again, Dad! I pretended to be suddenly deaf, to go along with my nonworking mouth.

Mom moved closer to the box.

Th-th-th-th-th, Norman snickered, in his Frenchy robot way.

Mom dipped her head so she was inches from the box, and pushed aside peanuts and straw, searching for the source of the weird sound.

That was when Norman launched himself at my mom in a burning rockets way, wrapping his arms around her and plastering her with kisses. *"Maman!"* he said, in between kisses. *Maman* means "Mother" if you're a French person.

My mom totally wigged out.

"Ah! Get it off of me!" she said, clawing at Norman as he planted kisses all over her face. "Someone help me!"

It was too funny—Dad stood there looking horrified, while Mom looked like she was wrestling with a love-struck octopus. But then it quickly got unfunny.

Mom pried Norman off and flung him away from her. The robot landed on the couch before falling onto the rug, so he wasn't badly damaged, but one of his eyes came loose, rolling across the floor and stopping near Dad's "captain's chair." The chair is designed to look like Captain Kirk's chair from *Star Trek*. It's not very comfy. Only Dad sits on it.

The sight of the rolling eye didn't calm Mom down, and was making me feel weird about my own eyes and if they were properly stuck inside their sockets, and how would a kid even check such a thing? Norman was in a heap on the floor, like an unloved doll.

Mom gave Dad the kind of look that, if her eyes were lasers, he'd have twenty holes burned into him. "What have you done *this* time?" she demanded. Her lower lip quivered, and I thought she might be on the edge of losing it. Why was my mom so upset about Dad's latest gadget? I wondered, completely clueless.

Before Dad could say anything—I think his mouth was malfunctioning too—Mom stomped across the living room, down the hallway, and into the home office, where she closed the door with a loud *wham!*

Dad sighed, tapped his fists against each other, and slogged to the office, where he tried to talk my mom into unlocking the door so they could chat. But Mom was giving him the silent treatment.

I gazed at Norman, who was folded in half on the floor, one of his fans whirring. I didn't know if he was programmed to feel sadness, but boy, did he look like a sad little robot.

"It will be okay," I told him, but in my head I was seeing him being shipped back to France first thing in the morning.

Maybe that would be for the best, I thought, ditching Norman before he could cause any more trouble. But he looked so darn sad. And he had looked so happy when he saw my mom. . . . I just wasn't sure what we should do.

10.

A minute later, after a tremendous amount of whirring and a few dozen clicks, Norman crawled into his box and settled among the foam peanuts and straw. He was still missing an eye; inside the empty socket I could see red and blue wires and what looked like part of a circuit board. It was like seeing someone's guts. I didn't like it.

"Maman does not approve of me," the robot said. "Scanning . . . scanning . . . scanning . . ."

And again. "Maman does not approve of me. Scanning . . . scanning . . . scanning . . ."

And again. "Maman does not approve of me. Scanning . . . scanning . . . scanning . . ."

I guessed that Norman was searching his data files for information that might help him understand why his mother, according to his programming, had pushed him away. I thought I should say something.

"I'm sure Mom approves of you, it's just that . . ." That sentence started out smart, but then it turned dumb on me. ". . . girls are weird." Yes, girls are weird, but that's not exactly news, and those words didn't help Norman. I had failed my first test as the big brother. Big brothers are supposed to be able to say smart things when needed. Not that I really thought of robo-boy as my brother . . .

But I guess it didn't matter, because Norman found what he was looking for in his database.

"In the animal kingdom," he said, in a voice that sounded tinny, "mothers will sometimes reject their offspring, especially the runt of the litter, if they believe that the offspring will not survive until adulthood. This evolutionary adaptation provides two benefits. First, the mother will not have to bond with a newborn that may only be around for a short time. Second, a limited food supply can be distributed to the offspring more likely to survive, while being denied to the doomed runt, perhaps ultimately hastening its premature death."

The robot peered at me with his good eye. "Am I a runt?" he asked. "Did Maman reject me because I will soon be gone? I would like the truth, Matthew, *s'il vous plaît.*"

The day was in danger of becoming like one of those shows on Animal Planet where the mama giraffe rejects the skinny little baby giraffe, leaving it to survive on its own. I hate those shows! I always wish the rejected kid good luck, and that he not get eaten by a lion. And then a lion eats the poor runt, even though the cameraman filming the horror could have stopped it if he had wanted to. Stupid cameraman. Save the baby giraffe next time, jerkwad!

Sorry. I just get so upset when people turn away from animals and people that need help.

"You're not a runt, you're a strong, healthy kid," I said to Norman. "If anything, I'm the runt. And this is the people kingdom, and the robot kingdom, not the animal kingdom. We do things differently around here."

"Logic error," Norman said, his body shaking like he wasn't built to handle logic errors. "You have been accepted by Maman and I have been rejected. Therefore, logically, I am the runt."

I didn't feel like arguing about which one of us was runtier, so I fetched the runaway eyeball, hoping that getting his eye back would make Norman feel better about himself. I stuck the eyeball in its socket, which made my guts a little twisty. Dad would tighten the eye later, but for now it was still loose, rolling around in the socket. More freakiness to deal with on a day already stuffed to the max with it.

"*Merci, mon frère,*" Norman said, the lens in his good eye zooming in and out like he was trying to adjust to having only one working eyeball. "Now restore the lid to my box, *s'il vous plaît.*"

"But . . . you'll be in the dark in there!"

"*Oui,*" he said. "I believe it would be for the best."

But I didn't think it would be for the best, so I told

Norman that we should wait until Dad came back—he'd know what to do. Dad was still trying to talk Mom into coming out of the office. It was sounding like it might take a while.

That was when Norman powered down. He wasn't in sleep mode—no blinking lights underneath his eyelids—but he was completely shut off. If I had known where his power button was I would have rebooted him, and he probably would have turned himself off again, and I would have rebooted him, and on and on.

See, with Norman turned off I could better hear Mom and Dad squabbling.

"Please, honeycakes, just give Norman a chance," Dad said, from the hallway.

"I am not a cake, honey or otherwise," Mom said, from the office. "Either the machine goes or I go."

Not having a way to power down like Norman did, I turned on the TV and cranked up the volume.

11.

I'd like to tell you something cool about my parents: The only reason they met was because a bus in France never showed up.

My mom had gone to Paris with several students from City College, which is where she got her bachelor's degree in sociology. She spent the entire summer in France, taking classes and seeing the sights.

One day Mom and the other students left their hotel and headed to a bus stop because they wanted to go to an art museum. After a half hour of waiting, Mom stopped a man walking by and asked if he knew why the bus was late. The man told her that the bus drivers in Paris had gone on strike, so there wouldn't be any buses that day.

The man's name? Matthew Rambeau, my future dad. Mom said she asked him for help out of all the people strolling by on the sidewalk because he looked smart and goofy, and people who are both smart and goofy almost never cause any trouble.

That sounds true.

Anyway, my future dad offered to drive my future mom and as many students who could fit inside his little blue car to the art museum. Once they got there my dad joined the tour, and when they were done he drove my mom and the rest of the students back to the hotel.

Sometime during that day they must have fallen in love, because my future parents spent the rest of the summer together, at least when Mom wasn't in class and Dad wasn't working at his job at a computer store.

But then it was time for Mom and the rest of the students to return to New York. And even though my mom didn't have much money, and the new semester at City College was about to start, and her parents wanted her to come home, my mom decided to spend another year in Paris. It was the biggest risk she ever took, Mom says when she tells this story, and she's glad she took it. My mom and dad got married that December and spent two years living together in France before moving to the United States.

It freaks me out when I think about it, but I probably wouldn't be here if the bus drivers in Paris hadn't been on strike that day, because my parents would never have met. That's also true if my mom had decided to play it safe and return home with the other students: She and my dad might never have seen each other again. Who knows what my dad would be doing now if he hadn't met my mom that day. Maybe still working at the computer shop in Paris.

But sometimes I think of it in a different way. Is it possible that every bus driver in Paris, or at least the guy who had the route that ran in front of the hotel my mom was staying at, went on strike that day so my future parents could meet? I know it sounds like a crazy idea, but all of us, I think, do stuff every day where we can't explain the reasons why we did those things. I know I do! Maybe sometimes we do this thing instead of that thing so some really cool things can happen, like two people meeting and falling in love, even if we didn't know that was the reason we did that thing.

Hey, it could be true. I'm pretty sure I owe my life to a bus driver in France who decided to join the strike instead of doing his job. Thanks, guy, or lady.

12.

Okay, on to more dumb stuff.

Mom finally came out of the office, and we had a family meeting at the dining room table. Family meetings are always about bad things, but fortunately this one had nothing to do with my grades or my lazy behavior, or Mom and Dad's "expectations" for my first year of middle school. No, this meeting was all about Norman. I was just hanging out, making sure I wasn't fidgeting too much so the meeting didn't suddenly become about my fidgeting.

Norman, Mom, and I sat at the table while Dad paced and told his side of the story, trying to win over Mom. The robot sat perfectly still next to me, but his eye, the good one, kept shifting between me and Dad and Mom. Each time his eye moved there was a mechanical *rrrmmph* sound. I think it made Mom nervous. She refused to look at Norman and kept letting out these weird little sighs like she was venting something big, bit by bit.

"If we can look at this with clear heads and open minds," Dad said in the voice he uses when teaching his classes, "then I'm sure we will agree that Norman joining this family will not only benefit us, but will also greatly benefit science, especially the fields of robotics, cybernetics, and artificial intelligence."

Mom, who had agreed to stay quiet while Dad said his piece, grumbled. I guess that wasn't cheating.

Dad said some things I already knew, that he and my uncle Jean-Pierre had designed and coded Norman and a second robot. And then he said some stuff that totally caught my attention, like that the existence of Norman and the other prototype was "top secret," and that there was only a handful of people in the world who knew they existed: Mom, Dad, and me, my uncle and his girl-friend, and two assistants who helped assemble the bots.

"What's the name of the other prototype?" I asked, jazzed about being involved with something that was top secret.

"Your uncle named him Jean-Pierre Junior," Dad said.

Big surprise! What's with the men in Dad's family naming their kids and robots after themselves? There are a thousand names to choose from!

Dad then said more stuff I didn't know, like that the plan was for the robots to spend a year with their host families as an adopted son, to see how they responded to family life, and how the families responded to having a robot as part of their family.

"We will tell everyone that Norman is a child we adopted from France, and we will treat him like a family member," Dad said. "It will be the exact same experience for Jean-Pierre Junior in France."

A fan whirred inside Norman, and it looked like a smile was starting to creep up the left side of his face. But on Mom's face there was nothing close to a smile.

"It won't work," she said in an irritated voice. "As soon as anyone sees that thing they'll realize something isn't right. The jig will be up."

Norman lost his half smile.

"I don't think that's true, Connie," Dad said. "Just look at him!" He glanced at Norman's wonky eye. "Well, except for that eye, which I can fix. That aside, Jean-Pierre and I have done everything possible to make sure the prototypes have the appearance and personality of a twelve-year-old boy. Frankly, I think we've done a remarkable job, especially considering that Norman and Jean-Pierre Junior are the first-ever artificial, genetically enhanced, cybernetically integrated, bionically modified life-forms."

I glanced at the robot and decided that my dad was right. If it wasn't for the fan and other mechanical sounds, and, well, the messed-up smile and the wobbly eye, Norman could pass for just another kid.

"But if someone realizes that Norman or Jean-Pierre Junior *is* an artificial life-form," Dad said, "and we can't talk them out of going public, then that will be part of the learning experience. I believe it's a risk worth taking."

Mom mumbled, "Maybe for you it is," and rubbed her forehead. It looked like she was getting a headache.

"What will happen after the year is over?" I asked.

Dad gazed at me. "In one year your uncle and I will meet in Paris to compare notes," he said. "If we believe that our robots are ready for family and social life, we will let the world know about our research and the two prototypes, assuming we also believe that the world is ready to integrate robots into the fabric of family and social life. I think all these questions will be answered by the end of the first year."

"Norman will keep living with us after the year is over?" I pressed. Mom was shaking her head sternly. A silent vote to send Norman packing, I think.

Dad told Norman to shut off his hearing.

The robot said, "Hearing interface is *débranché.*" Or at least that was what he said he did. Who knows if he was spying on us with his ears.

"You must understand, Matt," Dad said, pacing, "that in all fields of technology a year is a very long time. One year from now Norman and Jean-Pierre Junior, or rather their hardware and software, will be outdated.

It's possible we might be able to buy some time with a series of updates, but more likely they will need to be scrapped and replaced by newer models."

"You're going to kill Norman and Jean-Pierre Junior?" I asked. No wonder he had Norman turn off his ears. The poor kid was doomed!

"No, not kill," Dad said. "'Mine' or 'harvest' would be the better word. We will salvage what we can from Norman and Jean-Pierre Junior and build new, better models. Of course all memory and image files will be transferred to the new Norman and Jean-Pierre Junior, so there will be considerable continuity. But aside from hair and nails, your uncle and I have not figured out a way to make robots grow, or age."

"Its hair and nails will grow?" Mom said, gaping at my dad. "That's . . . creepy!"

"Creepy is the new cool," Dad said, smiling big like he was hoping to set off a round of smiles, but that didn't happen. Mom looked to be all out of smiles, Norman didn't hear him, and I was worrying about the robot being "harvested" a year from now.

"While Norman's hair and nails are technically synthetic," Dad said, "we were able to achieve growth by infusing the material with human DNA and RNA. If all goes well, Norman's hair and nails will grow at the same rate as Matt's."

"Well, that *thing* better know how to cut its own hair

and trim its own nails," Mom said, casting a glance at Norman. "I'm *not* doing that."

"You won't have to," Dad said, clearly getting more and more depressed at how the meeting was going. I try not to take sides when Mom and Dad are squabbling, but this time I was 100 percent on Dad's side. He and my uncle had done groundbreaking work in human robotics, and we were arguing about who was going to trim Norman's fingernails!

Then again, I hoped it wasn't going to be me. I don't even like cutting my own nails. It just feels . . . girlish.

What happened next. . . . Oh yeah. Dad told Norman it was okay to reactivate his hearing, and told him again when Norman didn't respond. It was brilliant me who told my dad that the reason Norman didn't turn on his ears when ordered to do so was because he couldn't hear his words. Duh! My dad is supersmart, but sometimes it's the dumb kind of smart. I don't know how many times he's left the apartment, headed to his job at the college, only to return ten minutes later because he forgot his briefcase, or his keys, or he remembered it was a Saturday and there were no classes.

And even though Dad could probably repair any broken computer ever invented, Mom will no longer let him anywhere near our appliances when they are on the fritz. This is due to Dad frying the fridge's motor last year while trying to fix it. The extra jolt of electricity blew out a wall socket, too. Mom made me call over my friend Jeter so we could devour all the Popsicles and ice cream before they turned into uneatable puddles. That was great!

Anyway, Dad was about to reboot Norman, but I told him to hold on a sec. I got Norman's attention, pointed to my ear, and gave the thumbs-up. The robot smiled, said, "Hearing interface engaged," and turned on his hearing.

Success!

"See, Norman is already learning," Dad said, "specifically interpreting a hand signal from Matt as meaning that he should activate his hearing. Fantastic! Norman has only been here for an hour and we've already had a breakthrough."

But Mom was not impressed.

"I saw a voice-activated toaster in the Neiman Marcus catalog," she said in a growly kind of way. "And a coffeemaker that will tell you when the coffee is ready. You of all people should know that computers can't learn. They simply respond as programmed."

Dad went back to pacing, but in a small circle, like a dog with a short leash. He gazed at Mom and nervously played with his tie. "So what do you think, sweet plum, are you ready to have Norman join the family as our adopted son? In the name of science?"

A nuke was about to go off—I could feel it. I wanted to hide under the table, say my prayers, and cover my head.

"I am not a plum, or any other kind of fruit," Mom said, glaring at my father. Their eyes locked, then Mom sighed and slightly shook her head. "The machine can stay for one month, and not a day longer. They say you can survive anything for a month. When thirty days have passed, he can go live with Jean-Pierre in Paris. And don't try to change my mind. That's my final decision. One month and Norman is gone."

"Great! Great!" Dad said, smiling in a way that made me certain he was going to do everything in his power to change Mom's mind before the month was out. He'd probably ask for my help, telling Mom how wonderful it was that Norman had joined the family. Heck, I might even learn lots of French from the kid. For a little cash I was willing to play along.

"*Excusez-moi,*" Norman said. "But I wish to let you know that I will be an efficient, well-behaved son for however long you allow me to stay here."

Mom faked a tiny smile in Norman's direction but didn't change her mind about how long he could stay with us.

I felt bad for Norman. First, he had been rejected by the woman who he thinks is his mother. Second, a month from now he will have to say good-bye to us and be shipped to France. Third, in a year he is probably going to be "mined" and rebuilt.

Poor Norman.

Mom stood up like she was about to leave, but she was stopped by a question from my dad. "Do you have any specific concerns about Norman?" he said. "Are you worried that a malfunction might cause him to act in a harmful way? Because if that's your concern, I can assure you there is no cause for worry."

Mom's anger seemed to drop away, but it was quickly replaced by something even worse: sadness. The body-shaking kind.

"Matthew, you just don't get it, do you?" she said, her words coming out a little fast. "Can't you see that it looks exactly like . . ."

Time out! I was expecting Mom to say that the robot looked exactly like me, but that's not what she said. Wait, I'll back up a few words.

"It looks exactly like Lucien would have. . . ." Mom's voice broke down completely. "Matthew, how could you do this to me?"

Crud! The story of Lucien is the saddest story in the whole world. I was hoping to not tell it, ever, but now you're wondering, so I guess I'll have to. Not yet, but soon.

Trying to stifle a sob, Mom hurried to their bedroom and closed the door. But the sob let loose when she was inside—I could hear it. Dad looked stricken, and I felt like folding myself into a little ball and staying that way for a long while. Norman? He looked puzzled, like an important bit of data was missing from his files.

"Scanning . . . scanning . . . ," the robot said. "There is no one in my family database named Lucien. Scanning other databases . . . Is Maman upset about something involving Lucien Bonaparte, younger brother of Napoleon Bonaparte?"

No, Norman, that wasn't it. But Dad and I just couldn't find the words to tell Norman about Lucien. *Our* Lucien.

13.

Warning: These next words are going to be sad. There's nothing I can do to make them happy. Sorry.

Okay. Here we go.

If everything always worked right, I would have an older brother named Lucien. He would be almost fourteen. He'd probably tease me about stuff, attack me when I'm sleeping, and brother junk like that. And I'd love it all, while pretending that I hated it, and attack him back whenever I had a chance.

Lucien—Mom chose his name—was born ten months after my parents were married in France. He was born way too soon and was messed up on the inside. He couldn't breathe on his own for a while, so a machine had to do that for him. Some of his organs didn't work right, so the poor kid spent more time in the hospital than he did at my parents' little apartment in Paris.

Mom and Dad tried very hard to fix Lucien, took him from doctor to doctor, but there wasn't much they could do except give him drugs for pain. My mom wasn't sure if Lucien really needed much pain relief, though. Even though he was screwed up, Mom said Lucien was almost always a "happy camper," hardly ever cried or raised a fuss. At least she used to say those things when she talked about Lucien. It's been a while.

Lucien lived for only fifteen months. Barely had time to look around at the world. He's buried in a cemetery in Paris called Gentilly. I've never been to France, so I haven't yet visited Lucien, my one and only real brother.

Mom and Dad were planning to stay in France and raise a family, but after Lucien died they decided to start over in New York. They moved here, and eventually I was born. My parents were very happy that I turned out normal. Or, you know, normal enough. And then they decided that having one kid was plenty.

There used to be a big photo of Lucien on the wall in the hallway. But one day about two years ago it went missing. I guess Mom and Dad got tired of seeing Lucien's picture each time they walked down the hallway. I can understand that, but I also think that kids who lost a brother they never met think differently than parents who lost a son. I keep a small picture of Lucien in

a shoe box underneath my bed. I can't imagine ever getting rid of that picture. What if I forgot what Lucien looked like?

So that is the story of Lucien. It's the saddest story I know.

And now you might understand why my mom was so upset when she saw that Norman looked a lot like Lucien would have looked if he had been born normal, or if there had been a way to fix him and he was still around.

Me? I don't mind that the robot looks like my real brother would have looked. Maybe seeing lots of Norman will make me think about Lucien more often. Fine with me. Even though Lucien wasn't around long, I really like that kid. He was brave.

14.

While Mom cried in her room, Dad, Norman, and I sat at the dining table, all of us stuck in sadness mode.

"I'm such an idiot," Dad finally said, shaking his head. "I can't believe I didn't see the resemblance. Idiot!"

I thought with extra might, trying to come up with a way to make Mom and Dad happy again, but nothing was showing up. I glanced at Norman. He looked lifeless, was maybe hibernating, though something, a wheel or a widget, was clanking inside him.

The day had turned rotten on us. And then it got even worse.

There was a mad pounding on the door to our apartment, like a crazy person was trying to get inside. And it *was* a crazy person out there: That's the way the terrible Annie Bananas knocks each time she stops over.

Annie Bananas is a girl who lives one floor below me. I wish it was a million floors below me, on the other side of the earth. Her real name is Annie Bonano, but I call her Annie Bananas to make her mad, and it used

to make her really, really mad, but these days Annie says it doesn't bother her. I hope she's lying. Making Annie Bananas mad is one of my major goals in life.

That's because Annie Bananas has been in love with me since the first grade. You'd think a love born in the first grade would have worn off a long time ago, but no, it's still going strong. Trust me, it's one-sided. I don't even like girls yet, especially the girly-girl kind of girls like Annie. She even has pierced ears!

And she wears fingernail polish!

And glittery lipstick!

And flowery dresses instead of a shirt and jeans!

Bleck.

Annie Bananas says that she and I are destined to be married when we are older and live happily ever after. The truth? I'd rather live with a gorilla in his cage at the zoo.

And even though I see her at school, and sometimes at the skate park, the library, the bagel shop, and other places, Annie Bananas stops over at least once a day, hoping we can have a "playdate." Not fun stuff like soccer or baseball, but dumb stuff like tag or the Princess and the Dragon (guess who is the dragon).

If Mom and Dad are home, I usually have to play with Annie. If they aren't home, I usually tell her to get lost. Or to go climb a mountain and send me a postcard when she reaches the top. I like to mix it up.

As the pounding went on, I moaned and groaned and looked at Dad, who, even though he always makes me play with Annie despite my protests, seems sympathetic about my terrible plight.

"Be brave, soldier," he said, pointing to the door.

So I stood and slunk to the door. When I was almost there, Dad said, "Hold on, Matt." He seemed to be cheering up a little. "This could be a good first test to see if Norman can pass for a human being. Invite your friend inside for a minute."

"She's not my—never mind."

I opened the door as slowly as possible and listened to Annie Bananas say, "Hi, Matt! I missed you *sooooooo* much!" We just saw each other two hours earlier at school! Anyway, I invited her inside, with as little enthusiasm as possible. Have you seen Mr. Smithers from *The Simpsons*, when his boss, Mr. Burns, is putting him in his place? I was Smithers—all grunts and groans and a look of total doom plastered on my face.

Annie followed me into the dining room and said, "Who is that?" when she saw Norman. "He kinda looks like you, Matt!" Annie likes to include my name in nearly every sentence that leaps out of her mouth. That bugs me in an attack-of-killer-bees kind of way.

"This is Norman, Matt's adopted brother from France," Dad said to Annie. "He's going to be staying with us for a little while." Hearing his name, Norman opened his eyes.

"Wow! Cool!" Annie said, all bouncy-bouncy. "But why did you adopt a kid all the way over in France? And where is his family? And how come—"

That was when Norman sort of flung himself off his chair, went to Annie, grabbed her hand and kissed it, and said, *"Bonjour, petite fille, comment ça va? C'est un plaisir et un honneur de faire votre connaissance."*

Annie giggled. "What did he say? I want to know what he said!"

I only knew what *bonjour* meant, so Norman had to do his own translation.

"I said hello, little girl, how are you?" the robot said. "And that it is a pleasure and an honor to meet you."

Oh brother!

"Say some more French stuff!" Annie insisted.

"Oui. I could say much more, pretty girl," Norman said. "Or I could do this instead."

The robot dropped Annie's hand and started doing backflips and front-flips and side-flips and flying barrel rolls, through the dining room and living room. It was impressive, but he was going way too fast, like a movie run at double speed. No real kid could move like that.

I thought for sure Norman had just blown the "Is he human or is he a robot?" test, but all Annie did was clap and say, "Wow! You're really good!" She turned toward me. "Norman is so cool!"

I gazed at Dad, who looked baffled, like he didn't

know that Norman could do the things he was doing. "You guys should go outside, get some fresh air," he said, aiming a thumb at the door. "Perhaps Norman can join you later."

"But I want to hang out with Norman!" Annie protested.

I knew what I had to do.

I bravely *bleck!* placed my hand *bleck!* on Annie's back *bleck!* and pushed her out the door. Norman, who was doing something I can only describe as a reverse cannonball off of the couch, his arms windmilling in opposite directions, didn't even notice. It was cool, but totally nuts.

"Your new brother is so talented, Matt," Annie cooed.

"Yep," I said, feeling vaguely annoyed by Norman's gymnastic skills. I can do a decent somersault, but that's about it.

As we stepped into the hallway we heard a crashing sound: Norman had accidentally flung himself into a wall, and his loose eyeball had popped out again. Annie looked back with concern, but I yanked the door closed. She must not have seen Norman's eye fall out or she would have freaked.

"Is he okay?" she asked.

"Don't worry. He's fine," I said. "It's almost like he's made out of steel." That was said as a joke, but later I learned that Norman's "protective shell" beneath his fake skin is made out of steel and titanium.

But it's still not later yet.

*   *   *

Having survived the elevator ride alone with Annie, we stepped outside, onto the sidewalk. My building isn't fancy enough to have a doorman, but there are doormen up and down my street. When Jeter stops over we sometimes walk around, saluting doormen like they are four-star generals. The doorman at a building called the Edward always salutes us back. But that's not something Annie likes to do.

So she and I just sort of stood there, watching people stride by. In New York City, everyone is always in a big hurry to get somewhere, even if they don't know where they are going. Oh. Did I mention that it was October and kind of cold out? And that I forgot to put on a jacket? I *really* wanted to be back inside. Since I was being forced to hang out with Annie, I was hoping that her mom would suddenly appear and tell her it was time for dinner. That probably wasn't going to happen. Annie is one of those kids who is almost unparented. Her dad hasn't been around in years. Her mom is a cellist for the New York Philharmonic, but she's hardly ever home. When she is home, she likes to be left alone to play her cello. It's kind of sad.

Anyway, I was getting bored just watching people, so I decided to push the "Is Norman human or is he a robot?" test a little further.

"Did you notice anything different about Norman?" I asked Annie as casually as I could manage.

"I sure did," she said, inching closer to me, so I inched farther away from her. "He's more polite than you are, probably the politest boy I ever met." She inched into the area I'd just inched away from, so I retreated farther. "He knows how to treat girls with respect. You could learn a thing or two from him, Matt."

Well, that was annoying, and not the answer I was looking for. "Anything else different about Norman?" I pressed. "Think hard!"

"Oh yeah, his right eye looks . . . wobbly," she said, after thinking it over. "What's the matter with it?"

"Nothing serious," I said. "Dad—er, a doctor will tighten it later."

Before I could come up with more test questions, Annie said, "Chase me!" and took off running, back toward the parking garage.

I ran after Annie, fast enough that it looked like I was chasing her, but slow enough that there wasn't any danger of me catching her. Running, I found myself worrying about Norman, hoping he didn't break anything else from flinging himself into a wall, and wondering if Dad might have to order some parts from France.

And I thought about my mom, hoping she was done crying, and that she wouldn't stay too upset about

Norman. I mean, he's just a gadget. He's not a replacement for Lucien.

"If you catch me, you can kiss me," Annie yelled, running in a zigzag way and not caring who heard those ugly words. Kiss Annie? I'd rather smooch with that zoo gorilla. I slowed down a step.

15.

Dinner was stupid.

Mom, Dad, and I sat at the table, eating some kind of chicken, rice, and broccoli concoction that had been frozen until a few minutes earlier when it met the microwave. Normally we have either home-cooked food for dinner or carryout. This wasn't normally.

Even though Dad told us that Norman can nibble food, the robot wasn't with us. Besides the eye problem, he had bent his nose and loosened an arm when he wall-crashed, and was waiting for repairs in the workshop, or what I like to call the Mad Science Lab. That's where Dad tinkers with his computers.

Almost nothing was said during dinner, but there were a few tries.

"Perhaps I can alter Norman's appearance so he looks less like Lucien," Dad offered, spearing a sprig of broccoli and examining it like it was a lab specimen. "Change his hair color and eye color. Restitch his eyebrows. Putty his nose."

66

Mom was separating the chicken from the rice: She's not a big fan of overlapping food. "Don't go to the trouble. As long as it's gone in a month I'll deal with it."

Dad's small smile quickly morphed into a defeated frown, like he was doubting he'd be able to talk Mom into extending Norman's stay.

I slumped miserably. This should have been a big, happy day. The most advanced robot ever built was living with us—easily the most exciting thing to happen to us ever. But instead of being happy we were all bummed out and having trouble finishing dinner. It just didn't seem right.

After downing some mushy broccoli, I told Dad that even though Norman acted weird and had a loose eye, Annie hadn't figured out that he was a robot.

"That's great news, kiddo," he said. "We'll consider it a successful first test." I got a slow wink from him and a thumbs-up.

But my mom was skeptical.

"Annie is a child," she said, "and not the brightest of the bunch." Good point, Mom! "I think any adult with half his wits will be able to tell that the thing is a machine. I don't want reporters invading our building when they find out we have a robot living here that we are trying to pass off as a person."

"I'll make sure that doesn't happen," Dad said, going back to his miserable voice.

I thought about Mom's words and wasn't sure she was right, that an adult would more likely detect Norman's robotedness. I think adults will look at Norman and see just another boy. But when kids first meet Norman they'll study him, wondering if he's the kind of kid they might want to goof around with, or, if not, the kind they want to make fun of or mess with. (Or if you are a love-crazed girl like Annie Bananas, if Norman is the kind of boy you want to play kissy-kissy with.) They'll watch Norman's every move and listen to each word he says before deciding if he's their type of kid. If Norman is accepted by Annie and other kids at school as a human, he might not have to worry about being busted as a robot by an adult. Either a kid will figure it out or no one will.

Mom, Dad, and I quietly finished dinner. I wasn't dumb enough to ask if there was going to be dessert.

16.

After I was done with my homework, I headed to the Mad Science Lab. Actually, it's a studio apartment three doors down that Dad rents so he has a place where he's free to play around with his computers. He spends a lot of time there, which makes me think it is also an escape place for him, where he doesn't have to be a husband or a professor or even a dad. He's just a guy messing around with computers. I get it.

Dad was repairing Norman on the worktable. He had peeled back the robot's chest and was soldering a yellow wire to something that had a bunch of wires running to it in a cable. I saw springs and wheels and widgets and processors and motherboards.

"I haven't a clue what got into Norman when Annie was here," Dad said. "I didn't program him to be a flirt with the girls, so it must have been Jean-Pierre who added that. Your uncle was girl crazy when we were growing up, but I'm not sure we should be passing that on to the first generation of advanced robots, do you?"

"Nope," I said. "Especially being crazy for Annie Bananas." I wondered if robots could fall in love. Is love something that can be programmed? Like Dad says when he's typing code, "It's all about the numbers."

I then asked my dad why he and Uncle Jean-Pierre decided to build robots. I wasn't totally buying the "for the sake of science" explanation. There had to be more to it.

He put down his soldering iron and gave me his full attention. "Believe it or not, I started working on designs for a robot shortly after Lucien passed away," he said. "I saw what his death had done to your mother, and wondered what if I could build a kid who was pretty much indestructible, as long as I kept up with maintenance and software updates? A kid, Matt, who could survive anything the world threw at him." My dad thought about something and shifted his eyes. "It was just a fantasy at first, no doubt an unhealthy one, but I spent countless hours working on schematics for a child robot. Too many hours, actually—it wasn't fair to your mom."

Well, that made sense. Why not try to create a kid who could never really die? If a part blows out, just replace it. If he gets smooshed by a runaway bus, just build a new one.

"How long did it take to come up with the designs?" I asked, trying to sound like a colleague instead of a dumb kid.

"A long time," Dad said, part of him seeming to slip back to those days when Norman was . . . what, a few drawings in a sketch pad? A pile of code waiting for a processor to be built that could handle it?

"Over the years I kept going back to the designs," my dad said, "and made several modifications. I also began working on the programming. How, for example, would you code a sneeze? What about a smile versus a frown? It was all very challenging, and invigorating."

He leaned toward me, getting excited like he does when talking about computers. "At some point it went from an indulgent fantasy to hey, this might actually be possible. About five years ago I sent copies of everything I had to Jean-Pierre, to see what he thought. I truly believed that your uncle would respond that I needed serious counseling, but instead he quit his job and began working on the project." He threw on a small smile. "And the rest is history. Or at least it will be if everything works out."

While I was thinking about his words, Dad went to his computer, clicked on a file, and showed me some of the first sketches for the robots.

The drawings didn't look anything like Norman, but we all have to start somewhere. And the way Dad's eyes shone with hope while showing me the file, I wanted like nobody's business for his robot experiment to be a huge success. The biggest roadblock might be my mom.

But if she knew what I had just learned, about Dad's crazy dream of building an indestructible kid . . .

"Does Mom know the story about why you built a robot?" I had to ask.

Dad quickly shook his head. "I'll tell her someday, when she's ready to hear it. But lately, every time we talk about those days following Lucien's death . . ." He parked that sentence right there.

I asked him why he wanted to name the robot André.

"It was wordplay," Dad said, returning to Norman. "You know—André, android. Kind of silly, I guess. Norman is a more fitting name. The word 'normal' is just one letter different from Norman, suggesting that he is a perfectly normal kid. No reason to look twice."

Huh—I hadn't thought about that. But thinking Dad might like to have someone on his side, I told him that André was a kick-butt name. That was when we decided that André would be the robot's middle name.

I watched Norman while Dad did more repairs with a soldering gun. His power was off and his eyes were snapped shut, but weirdly it felt like the robot was with us somehow, and that he knew what was happening to him. Poor kid was having surgery without an anesthetic.

"Can Norman feel what you're doing?" I wanted to know.

"No, of course not," Dad said, setting down the soldering gun. "Even if he was powered up, he's not programmed to feel pain. Perhaps Norman 2.0 or 3.0 will have that ability, if your uncle and I can figure out how to artificially create nerves, but this Norman will never experience headaches or toothaches or belly-aches. If he falls off his bike and breaks a bone—I mean a support bar—he'll never feel it."

Lucky robot.

Dad grabbed a pair of needle-nose pliers and went back to work, attaching a green wire to a circuit board.

Suddenly Norman's body shook. "Just a little power surge," Dad assured me. "Nothing to be concerned about."

I looked at Norman. What if my dad was wrong? What if Norman *was* feeling pain or fear or *something* from the surgery? That would rot. So even though he was powered off and supposedly couldn't feel anything, I held Norman's hand while Dad was working on him. That's something a brother might do when his younger brother is having major surgery, even if the kid brother, due to no fault of his own, happened to be a robot.

The weird part? I think Norman knew I was holding his hand. Maybe even tightened his grip a little. Yeah, probably just my overactive imagination.

17.

I put away the dishes from the dishwasher, and then I had to take a bath. In the tub I sank under the water to see how long I could hold my breath: fifty-four seconds. But I was counting kind of fast, so it might have been closer to forty seconds.

After I changed into pajamas, I returned to the lab, running fast down the hall in case any neighbors came out of their apartments—it's impossible to look cool when wearing pj's—and saw that Norman was back together and powered up. He and Dad were having a video chat with Uncle Jean-Pierre and his robot kid Jean-Pierre Jr., though my dad and uncle were doing all the talking. Dad and Uncle Jean-Pierre chat on the computer nearly every day, like they are best friends who can't go more than a day or two without catching up. I like it!

And it was kind of fun, comparing robot to robot. Jean-Pierre Jr. had a narrower face and darker eyes and looked quite a bit like my uncle. Both robots were wearing their berets, and for a few seconds I thought of them as the Beret Brothers, and almost laughed. But then I realized they'd actually be cousins, which wasn't as funny.

"Hello, Matthew," my uncle said as I sat down close to Dad. I said hey, and noticed that my uncle's girlfriend, Véronique, was tootling around in the background. Véronique is, uh . . . well, I'll just go ahead and say it: BEAUTIFUL. I was always happy to see her on chat, even if I did turn into a nervous blob of weirdness! It happens.

My dad and uncle went back to talking about Norman and Jean-Pierre Jr., and repairs, software updates, and junk like that. I was sitting right there, but I might as well have been sitting on the moon. I felt even more left out when they switched to French. About the only word I recognized was Mom's name, so I guessed they were talking about Mom not welcoming Norman into the family with open arms.

It was getting late and I was getting bored, so I was about to tell my dad that it was time for Norman and me to go to bed, when Véronique threw down some kind of tool, said, *"C'est de la folie, de posséder tant de matériel de qualité inférieure!"*—I could only guess what those words meant—and slipped next to my uncle, pushing him and Jean-Pierre Jr. aside so it was mostly her face on the screen. It was not a happy face. But then she peered at me on her screen and threw on a quick smile.

"Hello again, Matt," she said. "How are you this evening?" I noticed that she didn't say hi to Norman, even though he was sitting next to me.

"Um, fine," I said, squeaking a little. Something about Véronique's voice always wonked me out a little. So deep. So mysterious.

"I was about to complain to your father and uncle," she said, changing over to a mild frown, "about all the second-rate tools and equipment we own, when great wealth—and new tools!—could be ours if we went forward with news about our advances in human robotics. We could even afford to build a decent lab. In my opinion, waiting a year to break the news is absolute idiocy. It would be like waiting a year to cash in a winning lottery ticket!"

"But darling," my uncle said to her, "we've already discussed how important it is to test how the robots react to family and social life, the pressures and daily demands. And that will take time. At least a year."

Véronique scowled at Uncle Jean-Pierre. "They are machines, not people, and they have been thoroughly tested. If they blow a circuit board, we put in a new one. If they assault a *chaton* for no reason, we tweak the programming. What more is there to test?"

I caught my dad rolling his eyes and quietly groaning. This was not the conversation he wanted to be having.

"Apparently I'm the only one here who wants to be *très* rich," Véronique went on. "We could charge fifty thousand euros per robot, and I bet both of you that we would have hundreds of orders just on the first day. We've invented the next great must-have gadget, and you imbeciles want to sit on it for a year. *Complètement ridicule!*" She winked at me, then aimed ugly looks at my dad and uncle before jumping up and stalking away.

That was majorly weird. But at least I got a wink from Véronique, and a smile. Zing!

On the screen, Uncle Jean-Pierre rubbed his face and sighed. "Sorry about that," he said. "Véronique has been moody lately. I suppose I should try to talk to her, get to the bottom of it. Good night, *ma famille.*" He cut the connection before any of us could say good night.

I looked at Dad. He shrugged uneasily.

"Well, that was silly," he said, clicking off the video link. "If we do go public in a year, Véronique will get her fair share of the prize money, if there is any, and all the recognition she deserves. But we never once discussed mass-producing robots this early, before all the bugs have been worked out. That thought . . . it makes me uncomfortable."

Dad went on to explain that Véronique was primarily responsible for choosing the materials for the robots' hair, skin, eyeballs, etc., and without her help the robots would probably look like machines instead of like boys. "I wonder what's going on with her," he said. "Sudden greed? A desire for instant fame?" He shook his head. "Humans! Too complicated to deal with, at times."

True, but we can't all be robots!

A big yawn overtook my mouth. "It's Norman's and my bedtime," I said.

"Norman doesn't need to sleep," Dad said, "though every night at midnight he will do a system self-check, empty his cache, and dispose of any clutter."

That was totally unfair. So I told my dad that if Norman was going to live like any other kid would live, he needed an early bedtime like the rest of us.

Dad did one of his speed thinks, then handed me the robot. I didn't feel like carrying or dragging Norman to our apartment—he's kind of heavy—so I set him down, and we tramped out of the lab. The robot was walking better now, no stumbles or hesitations. I wondered if Dad had made an adjustment.

"Matthew," Norman said as we neared our door, "is Mademoiselle Véronique not a nice person?"

"Uh, you mean because of the video chat?" I asked. "She was just upset about something. Girls get that way a lot. It's one way you can tell us apart."

"No, not that," he said. "It is just that I did not enjoy how she referred to Jean-Pierre Junior and myself as robots and gadgets when we were right there, listening. It may be technically accurate, but . . . I just did not like it."

"I understand," I said, patting Norman on the shoulder and telling myself to never call him a robot or a gadget to his face.

Once inside our apartment we scuttled to the bathroom, where Norman watched me carefully while I brushed my teeth, then he said he wanted to give it a try. I washed off my brush, put some toothpaste on it, and handed it to Norman. He moved his hand back and forth so quickly I thought he might wear his ceramic teeth down to nothing, or break the brush, but that didn't happen.

"*Très rafraîchissant,*" Norman said, smiling and showing his teeth. "Very refreshing."

"Yep," I said, enjoying my own minty feeling.

On the way to my room, which I guessed was now *our* room, Norman said, "Our father and uncle are brilliant men."

"Tell me something I don't know," I said, which the robot took as a command.

"Polaris, the brightest star in the Ursa Minor constellation, is a multiple star located approximately four hundred thirty light-years from Earth, with a temperature of about seventy-two hundred Kelvin," he said. "Or did you know that already, Matt?"

"Maybe I did," I said, not wanting to appear dumb, even if I was sort of feeling that way. Like, for example, what the heck is a Kelvin?

18.

A few minutes later I was on my bed, under the covers. Norman was on the floor, stretched out on top of my sleeping bag. It was like a sleepover, but the other kid was a robot.

Out of the blue, Norman started singing that French song that goes, *"Alouette, gentille Alouette, Alouette, je te plumerai."* Hey, my dad used to sing that song to me when *I* was little! Having nothing better to do, I joined in the singing.

"Alouette, gentille Alouette, Alouette, je te plumerai."

I didn't know what the words meant in English, so after we were done singing, I asked Norman to translate.

"It is a lovely song about plucking feathers from a lark and preparing it for cooking," the robot said. "First you pluck the head, then the nose, then the eyes . . ."

Gross. I was singing about bird murder and didn't even know it!

* * *

Norman was silent for a while. But I wasn't feeling the least bit sleepy, which wasn't too cool, since it was a school night. If I didn't fall asleep pretty quickly, I'd end up dragging myself to classes the next morning.

"Matt?" the robot said. *"Ma boîte me manque."*

"In English, please," I told him.

"Pardonne-moi. I miss my box."

"Okey-dokey, pokey," I said. Like Mr. Henley, my music teacher back in elementary school, used to say, "If all else fails, why not rhyme?"

"Yes, I really miss my box," Norman said. "I miss it with every revolution of my hard drives."

I got the feeling that Norman wasn't going to stop talking about his precious crate until I fetched it. So I stood, growled in Norman's direction, left my room, tramped into the living room, grabbed the spare set of keys from a hook, opened the door, and snuck down the hall to the lab, where Dad had moved the box to. Inside the lab I saw my dad sitting at the computer, writing software code, lots of numbers and letters and those arrowy things: < >.

"Hey, Dad," I said.

"Hey, rocket ship," he said, typing. "Problem?"

"Norman misses his box," I said.

"Ah," he said, like a robot missing his shipping box was a perfectly normal thing.

I grabbed hold of Norman's crate, dragged it through

the lab, down the hall, into my apartment, through the living room, and into my room. Norman saw his box and sort of flung himself into it. Straw and foam peanuts bubbled over the top as he arranged them over him.

"*Merci*, Matt," he said. "This is much cozier."

As I was going back to my bed, I realized that Norman could have gotten his own box, but by whimpering he was able to get me to do the heavy lifting for him. The stinker! But I couldn't stay mad at him for too long. He was learning how to be a kid.

Midnight. I was finally about to fall asleep when several lights underneath Norman's skin flashed, and he said in this weird robot voice, "Engaging system self-check . . . Engaging system self-check . . . Engaging system self-check . . ." And then he said all the things he was checking, the processors, the drives, the ports, and the thingees and the whatevers.

"Checking RAM module one of twenty-six . . . Checking RAM module two of twenty-six . . ."

Ugh! I covered my ears and flipped onto my side. It wasn't going to be easy having a robot for a brother, I realized. I might never sleep again!

19.

Norman showed up on a Tuesday, but the lucky monkey didn't have to go to school on Wednesday or Thursday or Friday. Dad kept Norman home so he could do some updates and modifications, like adding padding so you couldn't hear it when Norman's pinwheels were turning or when his fans kicked on. He also cut Norman's hair a little unevenly and put a tiny dink in the skin over one of his cheekbones so he wouldn't look too perfect to be a real kid.

When the weekend arrived, it was time for field-testing. Dad and I took Norman to several famous sights of the city. There were always big crowds at those places, so they made great testing grounds, even though it was almost like my dad was expecting that at any moment someone would point to Norman and say, "Eek! A robot!" But that never happened.

Our first stop was the American Museum of Natural History, where we saw the usual dinosaur skeletons. That's always the most crowded part of the museum, but everyone was too busy looking at dinosaurs to pay even a nanosecond of attention to Norman as he stared for the longest time at a *Tyrannosaurus rex*.

"If this creature were alive," the robot said to me, "he would wish to eat us, yes?"

"We'd already be eaten," I said, wondering why God made dinosaurs so big. Probably the smaller animals that lived back then wondered the same thing!

Norman thought for a moment and looked kind of disturbed. "But I do not believe that would be quite fair," he said, "being eaten in our prime by a beast of such limited intelligence, and us having no say in the matter."

Agreed!

Next we stopped at a majorly cool display on how spiders weave their webs (scary!), and then one about how gemstones are formed over millions of years (almost interesting!). After that we went into the planetarium and saw a show called *Journey to the Stars*. The animations were really cool, and it did seem like we were right in the middle of where stars and all that other space junk hang out.

And I learned a few things, like that the first stars were born thirteen billion years ago. Man is that old. And Whoopi Goldberg, the show's narrator, has a really nice voice. Not sure why I mentioned that . . .

Norman seemed to be even more woggled out by the star show than I was, like he was overwhelmed by what he was seeing and was trying to process it all. Me too, buddy!

After the show, Norman looked at Dad and me and said, "The universe is so very large, and expanding, and yet there are microorganisms so small you need a powerful electron microscope to see them." One of his nylon eyebrows rose up. "I'm not sure that the universe is . . . logical."

"That's pretty much my take," Dad said, smiling.

Our next stop was Central Park, where we walked around the park, climbed around Belvedere Castle, and played with other people's dogs (that's the best kind of dog, my parents like to say). While I was tossing a stick to a big, happy collie in a game of fetch, Norman came up to me.

"*Pardonne-moi*, Matt," he said, "but I do not understand the merits of this activity. The animal expends all that energy retrieving the stick and returning it to you, and his only reward is that he is allowed to chase the stick again?"

"Yep, that's how it works," I said. Norman clearly was not satisfied by my answer. The collie had returned the stick, so I picked it up and gave it a good toss. This time Norman outraced the dog to the stick, bent and snatched it up in his mouth, and dashed back to me, dropping the stick at my feet. No lie! It was hilarious!

"*Non*, I still do not get it," Norman said, wiping a piece of bark from his mouth. While I was cracking up, Dad scuttled Norman and me away from the dogs and their owners and other park-goers, mumbling something about how he hoped that what just happened with Norman and the stick didn't end up on YouTube.

That made *one* of us!

Next we hit the Central Park Zoo. My favorite part was the polar bears, even though they were actually yellow instead of white, like they needed a good bath. Norman's favorite part seemed to be the penguin house, though at one point he looked puzzled.

"These birds are exquisite," he said. "But having wings yet being unable to fly is just—"

"Illogical?" I asked.

"Correct," Norman said, still looking perplexed. Hey, I've also wondered about the flightless bird thing. It almost seems cruel, like giving a kid a really great toy that *doesn't work and never will work.* Cruel!

Dad and I were pooped from all the walking, but Norman still had a full tank of gas. Instead of going straight home, I bugged my dad into stopping at a diner, the one with all the girls who'd won the Miss Subway contest since, well, forever ago. It's kind of a corny place, but they make the best chocolate shakes.

I was sucking down the last drops of chocolate goodness, and my dad was giving me the "Stop making disgusting sounds" evil eye, when Norman said something that freaked out both Dad and me.

"I believe I would like to be a museum curator when I grow up," he said.

I didn't know what to say. It hadn't dawned on me until then that even if he survived getting scrapped, Norman would always look like a kid. He'd never grow taller, without major surgery. He'd never age. And that just seemed . . . tragic, to be forever stuck like that. It really shook me up.

Dad and I shared a *What should we say?* look. Even

though I was feeling totally weirded out, I forced a smile and said to Norman, "Sounds like the perfect job for you." Dad turned away, his face probably showing something he didn't want Norman and me to see.

For the first time I was beginning to doubt whether creating kid robots was such a hot idea. Not that Norman isn't fun to have around, but . . . I mean . . . what about *his* feelings about a being robot instead of a real kid? Did my dad and uncle ever consider *that?*

Man. Just when you think it's going to be smooth sailing for a while, life gets all complicated again. I definitely prefer smooth sailing.

On Sunday, Norman, Dad, and I hit the Museum of Modern Art, where we joined a tour and saw several seriously weird sculptures, a display of some of the first photographs ever taken—kind of fuzzy—and an exhibit where all the art was made from those wax lips you can buy during Halloween season: partly gross and plenty weird! During a quiet moment, Norman asked the guide if the museum owned any art from "the great French masters." He rattled off a long list of names, none of which I remember.

"Please be patient," the guide said, and soon enough we were in a room dedicated to the life and works of a French guy named Henri Matisse. The paintings were pretty cool—though some of the people looked a little bent and floppy—and Norman was happy, but by then I was bored, bored, bored. Now, a display of art created by monkeys . . . that might have been interesting.

As we left the museum, Norman lectured Dad and me about the life of that Matisse guy, information that the museum had neglected to include in their display. "That's completely fascinating, Norman," Dad said, not looking very fascinated.

Then my dad suggested, because it was such a nice day, going downtown for a quick trip to Liberty Park so Norman could see the Statue of Liberty. There was no danger of climbing around inside the statue, since it was closed for "routine maintenance." Good. I've been inside the statue twice, and both times it felt beyond freaky, walking around inside of a *person*, even if it was a gigantic person made out of concrete and steel.

The secret's out. I'm weird.

Norman was quite impressed by the statue. "How grand, how magnificent," he said, gazing at Lady Liberty. He then told Dad and me that the statue was designed by some guy named Frédéric Bartholdi and was a gift to America from "the great people of France," which I already knew, except for the Bartholdi part.

The robot, as usual, had more to say. "The inspiring neoclassical design—a tribute to Libertas, the Roman goddess of liberty—the ever-burning torch and the *tabula ansata* . . . Well, I think that perhaps we should

have kept the statue and sent you something a bit smaller." Sure, Norman. You French snooty snoot!

That was about it as far as our weekend adventures went. . . . Oh, we did have one "mission failure," as Dad put it. He had wanted us to take a double-decker bus back uptown so Norman could see even more sights. But we'd only gotten twenty or thirty blocks when the bus we were riding on conked out, and the driver had to call for a tow truck so the battery could be jumped. The funny part happened when Dad explained to Norman what was going on. The robot asked if he had enough spare voltage to recharge the bus's battery. Dad smirked and said we probably shouldn't risk it.

Well, I thought it was funny.

So we got off the bus, hopped inside a taxi, and did our own tour, seeing Madison Square Garden— "Where the Knicks like to lose," Dad said to Norman— the Empire State Building, and other places I've seen a hundred times. But Norman was excited, which was all that mattered. And you know, that was the best part of the weekend. No matter if we were at a park or a museum or were hoofing it down a sidewalk, Norman looked at his surroundings with the big, hungry eyes of a kid being let out into the world for the first time.

And that was pretty cool. It's not every day you get a chance to introduce someone to the world.

As we were riding the elevator to the tenth floor of our building, Dad said to me, "If anyone had been suspicious about Norman being a robot, I think we would have heard something by now. I consider the field-testing to be a major success!" He looked totally psyched. Norman was treated like a human kid by sightseers, ticket takers, bus drivers, and so on, no questions asked. That was *huge*. I hadn't seen Dad this happy in a very long time. We high-fived, and then, after we explained to Norman what high-fiving was all about, he got a hand slap from Dad and me, too.

"Such an odd, primitive, socially awkward ritual," the robot said, shaking his hand as we stepped out of the elevator. Party pooper!

When we slipped inside our apartment, Mom shouted a hi to us from the home office and said she'd be out in a minute. That was the one sucky thing hanging over the weekend like a dark cloud. We'd invited Mom along for the trips, but both days she said she had too much work to do. If it was just Dad and me, I'm sure she would have come: My mom loves going places on the weekend, in and beyond the city. But since Norman was with us . . . Well, it was kind of sad. And I just didn't know how to fix it.

20.

That Monday was Norman's first day of school. But before we could leave to catch the bus, Norman had to endure a final inspection and some testing from Dad in the living room. Dad was worried that a mechanical glitch or software error would keep Norman from being accepted by his classmates and teachers as a human kid.

"Say that your sensory feedback loops are providing conflicting information that is threatening to overheat your CPU," Dad quizzed him. "Do you do a self-reboot or do you ignore the anomaly?"

"If alone and there is time, I do a reboot," Norman answered. "If with others, I ignore the anomaly until I am able to privately do a reboot."

"Correct," Dad said, smiling proudly.

The testing continued. Meanwhile, my mom, on the couch, was watching the *Wake Up, America* show with hosts Kent Cunningham and Nancy Smart, and the weather guy, Fig Ferrell—deliberately ignoring us.

Jeez, what kind of name is Fig Ferrell? Fig, who always seems to have rosy cheeks no matter the weather, was standing outside the studio, surrounded by a big crowd of nutty people, mostly tourists, while giving the national weather forecast. "It will be a great day for ducks living in the upper Midwest," he said. "But if you happen to be human, you'll want to take an umbrella with you to work." Almost funny! Mom likes that show because it's shot right here in the city, but I hate it. Everyone's always too peppy and happy for so early in the morning. But sometimes I sit with Mom and watch the show anyway, for the good part, sitting with Mom.

On the other side of the living room, Norman was running through multiplication tables so quickly I couldn't keep up. Dad put up a hand like a stop sign and said to the robot, "You might want to pace yourself, kiddo."

"*Oui,*" Norman said, smiling. "I believe I am ready for school now." But then he patted his head and seemed concerned. "Has anyone seen my beret?"

Norman was wearing jeans and a light blue shirt, part of the pile of new clothes Dad bought for him at Macy's, but adding a beret would have Frenched him up too much. Kids at school would have torn him to pieces. That was why I hid it under my bed earlier that morning.

"You probably shouldn't wear your beret to school,"

I told Norman. "Some kids will tease you or call you names. But you can wear it at home all you want."

"I would not care about the teasing," Norman said. "My beret is part of my outfit. I enjoy wearing it."

"Well, the other thing," I said, "is that kids might make fun of me, too, since I'm your brother. They'll pick on me or push me into a locker—that always stings. I like to avoid those kinds of things when I can."

While Norman's Axiom 96 processor seemed to be cranking away, I got an icky feeling that I was being self-ish. The main reason I didn't want Norman to wear his beloved beret was so none of the kids gave *me* a hard time. Selfish!

"In that case, I will only wear it at home," the robot said, grinning at me. I nodded back a thanks, feeling kinda rotten.

"You guys better go catch the bus," Dad said, checking his watch.

Norman and I slung on our backpacks, but suddenly the robot looked nervous. Not sure why.

Oh wait, maybe it was because I told him about the bullies at our school, like Todd Horner and Blake Benton, who beat up the new kids twice daily.

And about the tar pits behind the school that smart kids get tossed into just for being smart.

And about how one unlucky kid each day is sucked into a heating vent and is gobbled up by a slimy twelve-armed vent monster and is never seen again. Norman believed every word! Sure, I'll tell him the truth eventually. But it's not yet eventually.

"Good luck, boys," Dad said, pushing us toward the door. "This could be a big day for science and human robotics. Remember to look twice before crossing the street, don't take candy from strangers, monitor and compensate for voltage irregularities—that one is just for Norman—and all of that good parenting advice."

"*Oui*, no candy from strangers," Norman said. "Thank you, Papa."

I was starting to hate it when Norman called Dad "Papa." Dad's name is Dad.

Mom jumped up from the couch and met Norman and me at the door, where she kissed me on the head and handed me my lunch sack. Norman also got a lunch sack, but no kiss. Mom hadn't warmed up to him at all.

"Have a pleasant day, Maman," Norman said with warmth in his voice, but he only got a "yep" back from Mom. I kind of felt bad for the bot.

Norman and I were clomping down the sidewalk to the bus stop. Even though our school, M209—also known as West Side Middle School—was only twelve blocks away, my parents thought it was safer to ride a city bus than to walk. That might be true, but some of the smells I've smelled . . .

"*Pardonne-moi*, Matt," Norman said as we neared the stop. "But are you certain that I cannot bring my box with me to school?"

Norman was still nuts for his shipping box. He slept in it and crawled inside it three or four times during the day for long stays. The box thing was something Dad had not been able to fix with software patches.

"Sorry, but your box wouldn't fit inside the bus," I told him.

The robot blinked a few times. "What if we strap it on top of the bus with safety straps? I am sure Papa has some he could spare."

It took a few seconds for my half-asleep brain to come up with something.

"Won't work," I said. "The bus driver is way too mean to allow something like that. He once threw a kid into traffic for belching. The kid got run over by six cars, eight taxis, and a garbage truck. Poor kid may never belch again."

Norman looked terrified.

Giggle giggle.

21.

It was a warm, sunny day, and lots of red and yellow leaves were still hanging onto the trees that lined the sidewalks on both sides of the street. But all that beauty was ruined by the sight of Annie Bananas running up to the bus stop at full trot.

"Matt! Norman!" Annie said, all hyper-like. "I was hoping to see you guys today!"

Annie threw some air kisses at me—I ducked—and gave a real kiss to Norman, on his cheek. Oops. I forgot to warn the robot about the importance of avoiding Annie kisses. It isn't just due to cooties. I think Annie could be venomous. A snake with lips!

"*Bonjour*, Annie," Norman said. "*Comment ça va?*"

Annie snickered and looked at me. "What did he say?"

I rolled my eyes. "He wants to know how you are doing."

"I'm great," she said. "I'm just glad *someone* cares enough to ask." She threw me a *Why can't you be more like Norman?* look. I just smiled.

Annie then asked Norman why he didn't start school last week, and why she hadn't seen him outside.

Norman blinked several times. "I'm afraid that I required multiple repairs and upgrades before I was ready to interact with the larger society."

Annie looked confused.

"That's how kids talk in France," I said, in a rush. "He meant that he had to go to the doctor and get some shots." For some reason I never felt bad about lying to Annie Bananas. In fact, I enjoyed it.

Annie slid closer to Norman so their arms were touching. She was flirting with a robot and didn't even know it!

"Are you excited about starting school?" she asked Norman. "I hope we have all the same classes!"

I know it sounds crazy, but I was convinced that some color left Norman's face. "*Oui*, excited," he said. "I just hope that the vent monster does not disassemble me on my first day, and that I am not thrown into the tar pits by boys in the upper grades. That would be *tragique*."

Annie narrowed her eyes and glared at me. "What exactly did you tell Norman about school?"

"Hey, I'm just trying to protect my little brother," I said, fighting a laugh.

On the bus, Norman and I snagged a seat in the middle. Unfortunately, Annie found a seat right behind us and was pestering Norman with questions.

"So what was it like living in France?" she asked. "Did you have a family or were you an orphan? What do kids in France like to do for fun? Did you have lots of friends? Would you say that you were very popular at your school, medium popular, or unpopular?"

Norman turned slightly toward Annie Bananas. "Life in France was quite invigorating. Thank you for your inquiry, Miss Annie."

That's right. During preparations for school, Dad told Norman to not say anything specific about his previous life in France, should kids or teachers ask about it. But Annie was clearly dissatisfied. She frowned and said, "That's not really an answer, Norman." Seconds later she tacked on, "Why do I think you're hiding a big secret?"

Uh-oh. I thought that I better come up with something fast or Annie would keep asking questions, and who knows what Norman might accidentally reveal.

So I quietly told Annie that Norman had had a difficult life in France, and whenever he talked about it he got really upset. She seemed to buy it, sitting back in her seat and looking concerned. Count it as another successful lie to Annie, but for some reason I didn't feel too good about it. I hoped that I wasn't losing my touch.

As the ride continued I noticed that several kids from my school were looking at Norman, whispering about the new kid. So far, no one had accused him of being a robot.

Norman was noticing the attention too. He stood and said, "*Bonjour*, children. My name is Norman Rambeau, and I am Matthew's adopted brother, from France. I am pleased to announce that today I will begin my middle-grade studies."

The kids look confused. That was *not* how twelve-year-olds were supposed to talk. Not even the ones from France.

The driver, a big guy with furry eyebrows, checked the mirror and said, "Hey, kid. No standing when the bus is moving."

Norman glanced at me. I pointed to the driver and dragged a finger across my throat. "Sit down or he might throw you into traffic," I whispered.

My brother slunk down as far as he could go in his seat without being on the floor. Norman might not be able to feel pain, but he did seem to know what it was like to tremble with fear. Could be fun!

Annie smacked me on the head. "Be nice to Norman," she said.

Ow. For a girl, Annie has a decent smack to her. I almost respect her for that.

22.

Norman and I stopped at the office to get his locker combination, and a note from Principal Jackson introducing Norman to our teachers. Dad talked Principal J. into giving Norman the same class schedule as I had, so his first days at an American school would be "less traumatizing." Between you and me, I wouldn't have minded having a break from Norman—he can be pretty intense. But no one asked for my opinion.

Most of the lockers were in the main hallway. When Norman saw them, his eyes lit up and a smile took over his face.

"Boxes!" he cried, peering at the long rows of lockers. "Hundreds of vertical boxes neatly lined up!"

I could see how Norman might make that mistake, but . . . "They're lockers, not boxes," I whispered, looking around, hoping no one had heard him.

"And one of them is mine?" the robot asked, bouncing on his toes. I was almost expecting to see fireworks shoot out of his ears.

We found Norman's locker, 207, eight down from my locker. After I showed him how to work the combination, he slipped inside his locker and pulled the door closed.

"*Ç'est merveilleux!*" came his voice through the vents at the top of the locker. "I fit perfectly. Bye-bye, Matt. Enjoy your studies."

"Uh, Norman?" I said, bending closer to the locker. "You're not supposed to live in those things. And we have to get to homeroom, like right now."

That was when the bell, the one that means, *You better already be in class, sucker*, rang. So I ran to homeroom, planning to check on the robot later.

After homeroom:

Me: "Hey, Norman. Ready to come out of your locker?"

Norman: "No thank you, Matt. Bye-bye!"

After English:

Me: "Come out of there, Norman, so we can go to our next class together."

Norman: "Sorry, Matt, but I have never been this happy before!"

If you say so, buddy!

After social studies:

Me: "Ready to come out of there, brother?"

Norman: *"Alouette, gentille Alouette, Alouette, je te plumerai."*

Whatever!

After computer lab:

Me: "Are you—"

Norman: "Bye-bye, Matt!"

After lunch I asked Jeter to help talk Norman out of his locker. Jeter's real name is Dylan, but everyone calls him Jeter because he sort of looks like that guy on the Yankees. But I don't think my Jeter will ever be a pro at anything. He's even suckier at sports than I am.

Me: "Hey, Norman. Come out of your locker so you can meet my friend Jeter."

Norman: *"Bonjour,* Jeter. It is pleasant to meet you."

Jeter: "You too, Norman. But why are you inside your locker?"

Norman: *"Tout le monde doit être quelque part."*

Jeter: "Huh? What did he say?"

Norman: "Everyone has to be somewhere. So why not here?"

Jeter shrugged. I shrugged. And then we slogged to our next class.

"Your brother from France is kind of nutty," Jeter said.

"Tell me about it," I said.

"I think I just did," Jeter said, scratching his head.

Sigh. Did I mention that Jeter is sometimes as dumb as gum?

After math class, I asked Annie to help talk Norman out of his locker. As you can see, the situation must have been desperate if I was asking Annie for help.

"Why is he inside his locker?" she asked as we headed to the lockers. "Did you stuff him in there, Matt?"

"Not my style," I said, hoping my brain would kick in and shoot out an answer. Um . . . Got it! "You've heard of claustrophobia, where people are afraid of enclosed spaces? Poor Norman has a severe case of reverse claustrophobia. It's a popular disease in France." Someone give my brain a gold star!

"So he's afraid of non-enclosed spaces?" Annie said, giving me a doubtful look. I nodded, trying to look super concerned about Norman.

When we arrived at the lockers . . .

Annie: "Hi, Norman! Come out of there so I can give you a big hug!"

Norman: "*Bonjour*, Miss Annie. There will be plenty of time for hugs later. Stop by early next week."

Annie: "And I want to give you a big kiss! Come out and get kissed, Normy!"

Me: *Bleck!*

Norman: "I will graciously accept your kisses in the near future, Miss Annie. Bye-bye!"

The class bell rang. Annie gave me an ugly look. "Norman has only lived with you a week and already you made him weird!" She stomped away.

Actually, it was probably just some bad programming.

After art class, I was trying to talk Norman out of his locker when Oscar, the fiftysomething janitor, slid up to me pushing a broom. "Is there a problem here?" he asked. I guess it must have looked a little weird, me talking to a locker. Maybe even *crazy* weird.

So I told Oscar that my brother was stuck inside the locker, and asked if he had some kind of tool that could open locked lockers. He rubbed his chin while gazing at Norman's locker, like he was professionally assessing the situation.

"I guess we could cut him out with an acetylene torch," he said. Yikes! Sounded super dangerous! "But

I might have a simpler solution. What's the combination?"

Didn't know, so I tapped on the locker. "Norman, can you tell us the locker combination?"

"*Oui*. Twenty-six right," he said, and Oscar turned the dial to twenty-six.

"Eight left," Norman said, and Oscar twisted the dial back to eight.

"Seventy-two right," Norman said, and the janitor started to . . .

"Hey, there is no seventy-two," Oscar said. "The numbers stop at forty!"

Th-th-th-th-th, Norman snickered.

Oscar scowled. "You kids . . . You're all a bunch of jokers!" He left, pushing the broom. Sorry, guy!

The bell rang. As I scooted to the library, I could hear Norman saying fake locker combinations. "Eight thousand two hundred and twenty-six left . . . *Th-th-th-th-th* . . . One million, seven hundred and twenty-six thousand, nine hundred and forty-three right . . . *Th-th-th-th-th* . . ."

He's such a riot.

After study period, I didn't bother checking on Norman.

And the same with science class.

But when school was over, I *had* to get Norman out of his locker. Otherwise, I would be in big trouble with Dad. I was the older brother. I was supposed to be responsible for the mechanical rat. Plus, there was probably a serious law about leaving kids locked inside school lockers overnight. I was too young to go to prison!

"Norman, it's time to catch the bus and go home," I said. Silence, so I added, "Your crate's at home, waiting for you."

"I'm fine, Matt," Norman said. "I'll see you tomorrow. *Bonne journée.* Have a nice day."

Wow. Not even the crate thing worked. "But it's just not normal, living in a locker," I sputtered.

"*Célébrons nos différences!*" he said. "Let us celebrate our differences. What's good for the goose is not always good for the gander."

True, but Norman and I weren't geese. It was time to scare the little creep out of his locker.

"All right, see you tomorrow, Norman," I told him. "Unless the vent monster eats you."

Norman bit. "Eats me?"

"Yep. Every day at this time he leaves his vent and goes searching for kids still in the building. He can even slither in through locker air vents. The sad fact is, there are no safe places to hide."

The locker door flew open. "I'm ready to go home," Norman said, scampering toward the main exit.

Am I good, or what?

23.

When Dad came home from work, I told him about what had happened at school, Norman spending the entire day inside his locker. The robot was nearby on the couch, doing a self-check of his hard drives.

"That's rather disturbing," Dad said, pushing up an eyebrow. "I didn't write neurotic capabilities into Norman's programming. How would you code a mental condition in something that technically does not have a brain or human feelings?"

He was asking the wrong kid. "I think Norman can feel fear," I told him.

"Not really," Dad said, half yawning. "Norman *does* have sensors and feedback loops that may elicit human-like startle responses if some sort of danger is perceived. Basically, Norman is protecting his drives and data from damage by running away from that danger or otherwise avoiding a threat, but he's not doing it out of fear. He's simply designed that way."

Huh. Norman's fear of vent monsters and bullies sure

looked like real fear to me. But what do I know? In third grade I was certain that my teacher, Ms. Marley, was from another planet. She was tall for a woman and had kind of a big head, and one time on the playground I saw her looking up at the sky in a sentimental, too-far-from-home kind of way. But, let's be real here. She was *probably* not an alien.

Dad went to Norman and instructed him to run a check for bugs and malicious code. So Norman did his "scanning . . . scanning . . . scanning . . ." thing, blinking his eyes in a rapid-fire way.

"I'm happy to report that all code falls within approved parameters," Norman said. He peered up at Dad, shrieked, "Papa!" and flung himself at my father, giving him several kisses.

"I missed you, too," Dad said, giving Norman a quick peck on his forehead and setting him on the couch so he could finish his hard drive self-check.

"Scanning . . . Remaining hard drive storage capacity is 8.141 terabytes," Norman said, rolling his rubber tongue. What a weirdo.

When Mom came home, and after hugs and kisses were out of the way—with me and Dad, not Norman—Dad said to Mom, "Say you had a client come into the center with an unusual problem: His son, or daughter, has a fondness for enclosed spaces, such as a closet or a . . . box. What would you advise that client to do?"

Mom frowned. "Is this about the robot?"

"It's a hypothetical situation," Dad said. "I'm wondering what you would say to that person."

Mom sighed. "Evidently, the child is finding comfort in the enclosed space that he or she is not finding in the outside world. It's a feeling-safe issue. The closet or box is offering that boy or girl a symbolic 'return to the womb' where all was hunky-dory."

"Yes, a safety issue," Dad said, nodding.

"This *is* about the robot, isn't it?" Mom said. "Great. I always wanted to counsel a machine."

"Yes, I'm afraid our Norman has developed a neurotic attachment to his shipping crate," my dad said, "and also to his school locker. It's bizarre, from a parental perspective. But from a scientific perspective it's fascinating."

"Bad code?" Mom suggested. "A loose wire?"

Dad shook his head. "Like you said, if it's a safety issue, I'm wondering if there are things we can do to make Norman feel safer. Any ideas?"

"Don't put this on me, Matt," Mom said, lasering up her eyes. "I didn't bring that thing into our lives."

That thing has a name, I almost said, but I learned a long time ago to keep my mouth shut during Mom and Dad "discussions." On the couch, Norman had finished his self-check.

"This has nothing to do with you," Dad said to Mom.

"But what advice would you give that parent, the one with the child who has a fondness for enclosed spaces?"

Mom took a few seconds to answer, and I was wondering if this was going to be the start of a long fight. My parents don't fight very often, but when they do, it usually lasts a while. That's one bad thing about having smart parents. They always have lots of clever things to say to each other, some of them mean.

"Obviously," Mom said, "the closet or box needs to be replaced by a more suitable object, like a toy or a stuffed animal. But the ultimate solution will happen only when the child, or thing, feels safer in the world."

"Indeed," Dad said, rubbing at his chin.

"Enough of this silliness," Mom said, carrying her briefcase toward the home office. "I have real work to do. You guys are on your own for dinner."

Dad went into the kitchen, searching for an easy meal he could fix for us. I peered at Norman, who was looking like one sad little robot.

"Maman still does not approve of me," he said, lowering his head.

"It's only been a week," I said. "She'll come around." But I wasn't sure that was true. It had been a week, and Mom could still barely look at Norman. No reason to think things would be different next week, or the week after that. And then the poor guy would be shipped back to France.

In the kitchen, Dad scanned the contents of the refrigerator, then closed the door and said, "How about I order Thai?"

I said back a lazy "okay," but between you and me I was tired of the stuff. We have Thai food, like, twice a week: when Mom has too much work so she can't join us for dinner, when Dad is working late, or when neither of them feels like cooking. It's Thai food overload! A kid can only handle so much banana sticky rice. . . . But since my parents like eating Thai I decided to stay quiet, except for a few grumbles. *Grumble. Grumble. Grumble.*

24.

After dinner, Dad, Norman, and I were in my room, standing over my old toy box, filled with action figures, sporting goods, and toys I hardly ever played with anymore.

"Okay, Norman," Dad said, "I'd like you to find a safety object you can use to replace your shipping crate and locker—something that, whenever you are feeling a bit insecure, you can grasp hold of and think safe, happy thoughts."

Norman, gazing at the collection of junk, suddenly shifted into hyper robot mode, grabbing the action figures, balls, and toys and flinging them across the room.

When the box was empty, Norman climbed into it, wiggled around, and gave us a huge grin. "Such a wonderful box," he said. "*Merci*, Matt and Papa."

My robot brother then closed the lid. Inside my toy box he started singing one of his Frenchy songs.

"*À Paris, à Paris, sur mon petit cheval gris . . .*"

Dad scratched his chin. "Stuff like this just isn't in the computer manuals," he finally said.

"Yep," I agreed.

25.

Soon it was bedtime for Norman and me. I was on my bed. Norman had moved back to his shipping box and was resting on packing peanuts and straw. The kid just has a thing for boxes. I'm not sure he'll ever be cured.

We spent several minutes talking about horrible Annie Bananas.

"*Pardonne-moi,*" the robot said, "but I do not understand your concern. Miss Annie is a pleasant and energetic child. Also, she does not reject me, which I find most suitable."

"But she's a girl," I said. "And the *worst* kind of girl: the kissy-face, won't-leave-you-alone kind. Trust me, bro, you do not want anything to do with Annie Bananas. Jeter, on the other hand, is a boy and a pretty good kid. If you're looking for a friend, try him. He can get stinky when he hasn't showered for a few days, but you'll get used to it."

"Processing . . . Processing . . . With all due respect, I do not understand why gender should be a factor in choosing one's friends. Should not cohesive personalities and the intellectual vigor of the subject be of greater importance?"

For a walking encyclopedia, the robot still had a lot to learn. It was time for some education.

"Pay close attention, okay, Norman?" I said. "It's like . . . It's like us boys are earthlings, and girls are Martians. Annie is the biggest Martian of them all, like their queen. And Martians and earthlings just don't mix. For one, they have green skin and antennas, and talk weird. Maybe someday we'll feel differently about girls, but for now, if you think of Annie and every other girl as Martians, even imagine antennas growing out of their heads, you'll be fine."

"Thank you for the advice, Matt," Norman said. "I will consider your words and make the appropriate adjustments in my behavior. But what about her kisses?"

"You like Annie's kisses?"

"*Oui.* For reasons I am not able to explain they give my voltage regulators a little charge."

"Yeah, okay," I said, kind of getting what Norman was saying, but definitely not wanting to talk about it.

A little stretch of silence.

"Matt?" the robot said. "Why does Maman still not accept me?"

Another subject I didn't want to talk about! "It's kind of complicated," I said, hoping Norman would let it go.

118

"I have an Axiom 96 quad-core central processor," he said. "I can handle complicated."

So I told him the long, terrible story about Lucien. Norman listened without interrupting me.

"The big problem," I said, "is that you look just like Lucien would have looked if he had stuck around. I guess it brings back some bad memories for Mom."

"Correction," Norman said. "*I* brought back the bad memories."

I didn't know what to say.

"Processing . . . What if I help around the apartment?" the robot asked. "Do chores and be of assistance to Maman whenever possible? Would that cause her to accept me?"

"Couldn't hurt." I'll admit that I'm not too helpful around the apartment, probably create ten messes for every one mess I clean up. If Mom or Dad tells me to put away the dishes or vacuum the rug, I'll do it without complaining much, but I never volunteer for those kinds of things.

To make sure Norman stopped bothering me, I closed my eyes and fake snored.

Snorrrre-frewwwww . . . Snorrrre-frewwwww . . .

"Matt?" the robot said. "Can you stop pretending to be asleep? I just thought of something."

Busted! "What?"

"If Lucien were here, he would be my brother too."

True. I hadn't thought of it that way before, but Norman should have two brothers, not just me.

Groan . . . scrape . . . groan . . . I think Norman was sobbing, in his own Frenchy robot way.

And my eyes started leaking a few tears for a brother I'd never met. And, as more tears leaked out, I thought about the crazy robot over there in his box, worried about Mom, sad about Lucien, and trying to find a way to cry.

26.

The next morning I was awakened, way too early, by Norman pounding on my bedroom door and saying, "*Bonjour, mon frère.* It is time for breakfast!" Then, down the hall, I heard him banging on Mom and Dad's door and saying, "Please wake up, Maman and Papa. Breakfast is served!"

What the heck was Norman up to? I wondered, stretching my arms awake. And, weird thought, just what might a robot serve for breakfast?

Mom, Dad, and I stumbled into the dining room at the same time and saw a table filled with plates of pancakes and waffles and turkey bacon, a basket of muffins, and pitchers of orange juice and organic milk. There was enough food for twenty people.

"Well, this is unexpected," Dad said, scratching at his chest and yawning.

"I feel fat just looking at all this food," Mom said. Note: My mom is skinny. If she owns any fat, it's hiding.

I had nothing to say. I think my voice box was sleeping.

A spiffed-up Norman—he was wearing a white shirt, black slacks, and a red bow tie (where the heck did he find a bow tie?)—said, "Please, family, take your seats so your new cook, waiter, butler, and maid may have the honor of serving you."

As we sat down, Norman forked two pancakes and one waffle onto our plates, gave each of us two strips of bacon and a blueberry muffin, and filled our glasses with juice and milk.

"*Bon appétit!*" the robot said, folding his arms behind his back. I suddenly got it. Norman was trying to win over Mom by taking over some of her duties, like fixing breakfast. I hoped it would work, but was doubtful.

"Thanks, Norman, this looks great," Dad said.

"Yeah, thanks a lot," I added.

It took Mom about ten seconds, but then she said a polite "thank you," without looking at Norman.

We passed around the bottle of maple syrup, then dove in, while Norman stood and watched us with hopeful eyes.

The pancakes were really tasty. My waffle, too. But I thought that I better not seem too excited or Mom's feelings might be hurt, knowing she had been out-cooked by a robot.

But my dumb dad . . .

"These pancakes are out of this world!" he said. "Best I've ever had, by a mile." He quickly caught his goof-up.

"I mean the best I've had since Connie made pancakes a few weeks ago."

"Nice try," Mom said. "But . . ." And here she actually stole a glance at Norman. "The pancakes are really great. Better than I could make."

"Thank you, Maman and Papa," Norman said, looking like he was about to drip tears of joy if he had that ability. "I accessed recipes from some of the finest chefs in Paris in order to prepare the best breakfast possible."

Dad set his fork down and looked concerned. "Accessed or hacked?"

Norman excitedly bounced. It was kind of cute. "I think that I better not answer that question, Papa," he said, shifting his eyes back and forth.

Mom, Dad, and I smiled.

Progress, I thought.

27.

An hour later Norman and I were at the bus stop, waiting for the bus.

"I believe that Maman was pleased with breakfast," the robot said, blinking.

"Yep," I said. "Plus, I think she liked that you cleaned all the dishes and pots and pans. You're better at that kind of thing than I am."

"Ah, but it is not difficult to change your behavior, Matt. If you make a mess, you clean it up."

"I guess," I said, not too eager to give up my lazy side—it's a big part of who I am. Plus, did I really want to be taking advice from a robot?

Oh great.

"Annie Bananas alert!" I warned Norman, as Annie ran to us like a starving monkey to a banana tree. When she arrived due to her not falling down a manhole—rats!—she tried to give Norman a kiss, but he pushed her away.

"My apologies, Miss Annie," the robot said, "but Matt

has advised me that due to complex social practices I was not previously aware of, we can only be non-kissing acquaintances."

He offered his hand. Annie shook it, then punched me hard on the arm. *Ow.*

"What did you do to my Norman?" she hissed, toxic spit molecules flying my way. "You ruined everything!"

"All I did was tell Norman the truth about things like cooties and girl venom," I said. That earned me another Annie punch. *Ow.*

That was when a mime—a guy in his thirties wearing white face paint and the usual outfit—slid up to us and started doing his routine, pushing up against an invisible wall. This is New York City. There is an ever-present risk of running into a mime.

I pretty much ignored the guy, and since mimes are really quiet that was easy to do. Only Annie seemed to be enjoying the show, clapping like a lunatic. Meanwhile, Norman elbowed me in the side and pointed to the mime. "Mechanical dysfunction?" he whispered. "Voltage irregularity?"

"Could be," I whispered back.

The mime started pretending that he was pulling an invisible rope. How original! If he kept at it, I thought I might flag down a cop and report the guy as being suspicious as part of the "If you see something, say something" safety campaign. Hey, you never know, the mime could have been strapped with pretend explosives underneath his shirt. He could have silently gone *ka-boom!*

While I was smiling at my own thought—I do that sometimes—a second man in his thirties, wearing a dark suit and holding a video camera, came up to us and said, "How wonderful, a mime!" He started taping the mime's performance, but then I noticed him aiming the camera at Norman and staying on him for several seconds. *Hmm.*

Do you remember the day you first realized that the scrambled eggs you were eating were, well, chicken gunk? And that the glass of milk you just guzzled down was meant for some calves, not you? And that sausage patty on your plate—well, you get the picture. And how you thought, while riding waves of oogliness, that maybe things weren't really how they seemed, that quite possibly it was a freaky-bizarre world you were living in that people only *pretended* was a normal world, but you at long last had discovered its true freaky-bizarre nature? Or something like that! Well, I was starting to get that feeling, watching the mime and the guy with the camera, that things weren't really how they seemed on the outside. But before that feeling could totally oogle me out the bus pulled up, and Annie, Norman, and I climbed aboard, leaving the mime and the dude with the camera behind.

Man, I hated being mimed so early in the morning.

I almost wanted to go back to bed, wake up, and start over.

At school, Jeter, Annie, and I had to stand in front of Norman's locker to block him from slipping inside and staying there until it was time to go home. But it worked, and Norman and I made it to homeroom just as the bell rang.

Homeroom is usually spent listening to announcements from Principal Jackson and catching up on homework we forgot to do. But when Ms. Purcell introduced Norman to the class and said he was from France, a ditzy girl named Wendy Callahan asked the robot to say something in French.

"Une souris qui n'a qu'un trou est vite attrapée," Norman said. "A mouse that has only one mouse hole is quickly caught. That is a popular proverb in France. It means, as you Americans say, better safe than sorry."

Some kids looked stunned and amazed, like Norman had just spoken Martian and translated what he said.

And then a chubby boy named Todd Grossman asked Norman to say something else in French, so Norman said it, and then more kids asked for French words and sayings, and before I knew it, it was time for our next class. Good thing I was caught up on my homework. It was way too noisy to get anything done.

*　　*　　*

In English, Norman spent the class translating Mr. Kelly's words into French as he lectured about social themes in *Huckleberry Finn* and read from the book. Show-off!

When class was over, Mr. Kelly thanked Norman and patted him on the head in a "good dog" way. Well, that stank. I never get pats on the head from teachers, and have never come close to being a teacher's pet. *Grrr.*

In social studies, Norman amazed the class by vocalizing his data file on World War I. That took nearly the entire class. "Wow, you're smarter than our teacher," a kid named Denny Sackett said. Several kids nodded. Our teacher, Ms. Finkel, didn't look too happy.

In computer studies, Norman fixed Jenny Huffleman's computer when it went berserk. Using a screwdriver he borrowed from the teacher, Norman took apart the PC, tightened this, adjusted that, blew dust off that thing, and *voilà*, it was working again. The class applauded, then Jenny gave Norman her phone number *and* e-mail address. "Call me, Norman," she said, smiling big. Man! No girl ever gave me her phone number and e-mail address. Not that I'd want that stuff.

At least lunch period was next. It would be impossible for Norman to show off at lunch, right?

*   *   *

On the way to the cafeteria, Norman and I passed by his locker without him trying to sneak inside it. So I asked Norman if he was over his "box thing."

"Matt," he said, in his serious robot voice, "during computer class I was able to access a blueprint of our school building and saw that it is, essentially, one large rectangular box, with several smaller boxes inside it, such as classrooms, closets, and lockers. So in many ways I am still in a box during school hours—several boxes, actually—but ones I have to share with my classmates. It is not quite as suitable as solitary box confinement, but for now it will have to do."

Okay then!

(Later I realized that Norman, the little devil, must have hacked into the main computers for the New York City Department of Education to see that blueprint. But it's still not later yet.)

Usually it was just me and Jeter at our lunch table, but with Norman there it was packed with a dozen kids, including the terrible Annie Bananas. Other kids stopped by to ask Norman to say something in French, or for help with their homework.

So it *is* possible to show off during lunch. And Norman was sure eating up the attention. But you know what I wanted to do? I wanted to shout to the entire school, "Norman is a robot! Of course he's smart and clever. He's programmed to be smart and clever!"

But I held my tongue. I didn't want to ruin Dad's big experiment.

And then the amazing Norman earned more love and applause by balancing a pencil on his nose. Huh. I could probably do *that*.

On our way to math class, Norman and I ran into Blake Benton, probably the top bully in the sixth grade. How mean was Blake? Rumor had it he once beat up an NYU student just for looking at him funny.

"It's the new kid from France and his idiot brother," Blake said, snarling. "We don't like French people here in America. Why don't you both go live in France where you belong?"

I was actually kind of happy that not everyone had fallen in love with Norman. But I also wanted to avoid suffering one of Blake's belly bams. They can take away your air for a full minute.

I tried to step past Blake, but he pushed my shoulder. "Where do you think you're going, Matt the rat?" he asked.

Before I could think of a smart answer, or a dumb one, Norman said to Blake, "*Pardonne-moi*, my aggressive classmate, but if you do not desist in your antisocial behavior, I will be forced to respond appropriately."

Blake snickered. "Oh yeah? What are you going to do, slap me like a girl? Like a French girl?"

"Non," said Norman. "I will just do this." In a blurry flurry he demonstrated a dozen judo and karate moves, rolls, flips, kicks, and hand chops. Wow! I didn't know he could do that stuff. The kids who had gathered to see a fight looked impressed. I was too. Norman was like a black belt karate dude, but speeded up. A robot Jackie Chan!

Blake suddenly looked pale. "I'm late for class," he said, hurrying away. A few kids laughed at Blake and cheered for Norman. As we headed to math, I thanked the robot for saving me from a belly bam.

"Happy to help, *mon frère,*" Norman said. "Like you say in America, I have your backside."

"It's *back,* not backside," I said to Norman. "A backside is a butt."

Norman turned beet red with embarrassment. It was just his programming.

In math, Norman quickly answered every math problem Ms. Porter and the kids tossed at him. $387,671 \times 56 \times 2,114 =$ no problem for Norman.

"Wow, you're as fast as my calculator," said a red-haired girl named Dahlia Simpson.

That's because he *is* a calculator, I almost said. But I didn't.

*　　*　　*

In gym, Norman stunned and amazed everyone by expertly doing somersaults, flying over the horse, and performing like an Olympian on the uneven bars, balance beam, and rings.

What a show-off! Between you and me I almost wanted Norman to fall, on the beam or the bars or the rings. Anything! I didn't want him to get hurt or lose an eyeball again, I just wanted him to not be so darn perfect. Was that bad?

In the locker room, I was starting to undress for a quick shower when I saw Norman sitting on a bench in his clothes, looking worried.

"Matt?" he said. "I am concerned that I am not fully waterproof, that exposure to pulsating water might cause said water to penetrate my protective shell and cause major damage to my processors and electrical system."

In my head I saw Norman sparking out in the shower room. Funny! I mean, *tragique.* So I went to Mr. Watts in his little office and asked if it was okay that Norman skipped taking a shower. "He has a bad water allergy," I said.

"Never heard of it," Mr. Watts said, "but it sounds like something they would have in France. Sure, if Norman wants to skip his shower, that's A-OK with me."

Great. But why did I suspect that if I asked Mr. Watts if it was okay for me to skip *my* shower, he would have said something like, "What are you, a sissy girl? Get in the shower, Rambeau!"

Totally unfair.

In study period . . . Actually, nothing weird happened during study period.

In science class, Mr. Chambers put Norman, "Our resident genius, I've been told," in charge of the lesson. Mr. Chambers has always been lazy, but I guess he was turning it up a notch. Or would it be *down* a notch?

Norman, standing at the head of the class, opened the science textbook Mr. Chambers handed him and lectured about the wonders of chromosomes and DNA for nearly forty minutes. Except for some brainy words I didn't know, it was kind of interesting. But it's weird, isn't it, how things as small as chromosomes can decide so much about who you are. I guess the same is true with Norman, but it's computer code making him who he is instead of the other kind of code. The *real* kind.

Finally school was done, and Norman and I were heading to our lockers to put away our books and grab our jackets.

I was thinking okay, Norman had a big day, did some

amazing things, but in another day or two it would wear off, and kids would start to get bored and would treat him like any other brainy nerd.

But when we arrived at our lockers, a few kids started chanting, "Norman . . . Norman . . . Norman . . ." And then more kids joined in. Soon there were like a hundred kids chanting my brother's name.

"*Merci*, classmates," said Norman, smiling and waving. "You have been so very kind to me. Because of this outpouring of kindness I almost forgot about the terrible vent monster!" Some kids look puzzled, but then Norman did a standing-in-place backflip, and they cheered and hooted.

If I tried a standing-in-place backflip, I'd break my head. *Sigh*.

28.

Instead of riding the bus home, Norman and I took a different bus to the Community Help Center, where my mom works. Once a week I help with the kids who show up for the after-school program. There's a gym, so there's always a basketball or volleyball or kickball game going on. Sometimes I organize the little kids into teams and act like I'm their coach. It's pretty cool.

Oh. Mom didn't invite Norman to help out at the center, but I thought it would be rude to send him home while I went and had fun. So I dragged Norman along, hoping it would work out okay.

When we went into the office, Mom, sitting behind her desk, glanced at us and said, "Oh, you brought *it*." She started tapping a pen against a pile of papers in front of her for a crazy-long time. *Tap tap tap tap tap tap tap*. Norman looked at me. I looked at Norman. *Tap tap tap tap tap tap tap*. And, to our surprise, Mom finally said, "I guess that's okay. Just try to keep him from causing any trouble." She waved us away so she could get back to her paperwork.

What a relief, not getting yelled at for bringing Norman along. But the robot looked hurt. And I didn't know what I could say or do that would make him feel better.

There was a basketball game going on, all boys, mostly fifth and sixth graders, which meant I shouldn't stand out as being too sucky, so I joined in. Norman sat in the stands so he could do some routine system maintenance.

I was with the "skins" team. It's always weird taking off my shirt in public and showing my puny chest. Someday, I tell you, I will be ripped! Anyway, shortly after I jumped into the game, play was stopped when one of the kids was bonked in the nose with the ball and looked like he was about to cry. Nose stingers are the worst. Waiting, I peered at the stands to see how Norman was doing. He was talking to a girl. Of *course* he was talking to a girl. He was *always* talking to a girl, like he was some kind of studster robot or something.

Then I did a double take. He wasn't talking to just any girl, he was talking to Robin. Robin didn't talk. I mean she could talk, but she never talked, *ever*, except to her parents, and then only sometimes. Robin is tiny and thin. I think she's eight. She has been coming here for as long as I have, and I had never seen her talking to the other kids, or showing any interest in what they were doing. Instead she just sat by herself and played with stuffed animals, or colored in a coloring book. It was kind of sad.

But that day, Robin was talking to Norman. And I wasn't the only one noticing.

"No way," said a tall kid named Tyler. "I never thought I'd see weirdo girl talking to anyone, ever. Who's the midget she's talking to?"

"My adopted brother," I said. "He's not a midget; he's nearly five foot two." (Okay, I measured Norman one day when he was in sleep mode. So sue me.) "He's from France," I added.

A few kids nodded, like Norman being from France explained everything.

"And, by the way, Robin isn't weird, she's autistic," I said, feeling strangely brave. But Tyler just shrugged. In his world, "autistic" and "weird" are probably the same thing. I like my world better.

Some of us moved closer so we could hear what Norman and Robin were chatting about. The stock market? Poisonous frogs? With Norman anything was possible.

As I strained to hear, I couldn't help but smile. Norman was teaching Robin a song, the one that went:

Frère Jacques, Frère Jacques,
Dormez-vous? Dormez-vous?

Sonnez les matines, sonnez les matines,
Din, dan, don, din, dan, don.

And then he taught Robin the English version, which I knew better.

Are you sleeping? Are you sleeping?
Brother John, Brother John.
Morning bells are ringing, morning bells are ringing,
Ding, dang, dong, ding, dang, dong.

The sight of Norman and Robin ding-donging together was pretty darn cute. It was choking me up a little. Seriously! My throat felt all clogged up.

That was when Mom and her assistant, Judy Goodman, busted into the gym. Someone must have told them that Robin was talking to Norman.

At first Mom looked upset, like she was ready to save Robin from Norman, maybe toss the robot into the broom closet where he couldn't do any harm.

But then, as Norman and Robin's quiet singing continued, something changed on Mom's face. She stared and stared, and then she swallowed hard. "Would you look at that!" she said to Judy. "I've been hoping to see something like this for the longest time."

"Never stop believing in the power of the human spirit," Judy said to my mom. (Or the power of the robot spirit, I thought.) Mom and Judy watched Norman and Robin some more, beamy looks on their faces. Judy is the kind of person who is always saying sunny things about miracles and happy outcomes. Fall off of your bike and scrape your knee? Judy will tell you about the cool scab that is about to form. I like Judy.

When the song was over, Robin shot Norman a quick glance that clearly said, *More.* The rest of us just watched, amazed, as, in his softest voice, Norman began another song, and Robin joined him. She was looking at the floor, maybe not used to all the attention, but she was still singing. Good for her!

Mom looked over at me with big, questioning eyes, but I just shrugged. I was kind of shocked too. A singing, happier Robin was probably here this whole time and we didn't even know it. But . . . Norman somehow did?

Norman and Robin were still singing when Robin's mother came to claim her. Robin's mom was so blown away from seeing her daughter singing that she started blubbering. She wasn't the only one. Mom's face was pinching up, which is always a big clue that she's trying very hard to not cry.

Robin whispered something to Norman and gave him a really sweet smile, then scampered to her mother. Poor Robin got a crushing hug: She looked trapped and a little uncomfortable.

As Robin and her mother left the gym, I went up to Norman and asked what Robin had said to him.

In a quiet voice he answered, "She asked, 'Batteries or wind-up?' Naturally, I could not admit to being battery-powered, since Papa advised to not say anything if someone figured out that I am robotic."

Holy fried bananas! Robin pegged Norman as a robot when everyone else he had met missed it? That was just—yeah, my favorite word—freaky!

"But how did she figure out you're . . . you know, mechanical?" I asked Norman.

Norman paused for a moment, like he was retrieving a data file. "When I first went up to Robin, she said, 'You must be a toy. Only toys like to play with me.' It would have been unethical to deny being a toy, since in a rudimentary way I am one, so I stayed quiet. But yes, Matt, the cat has finally jumped out of the hat, as you Americans like to say. Should we tell Papa?"

"Not yet," I quickly answered, deciding that mum was the word unless other kids caught on. Dad would have freaked for a week if he knew that someone had already discovered the truth about Norman. Not one of our neighbors, or a teacher, or any of the brainiacs at M209, but, sweet, quiet Robin.

Actually . . . that was kind of cool.

29.

Dinner that night was lentil and rice pilaf and a salad with lots of weird greens and radish slivers. It was almost as tasty as it sounds.

Mom was bubbly for a change, telling Dad what had happened with Norman and Robin at the help center. "It was pretty darn incredible," she said. "Judy and I have been working with Robin for nearly a year, trying to find something she'd enjoy doing, even if she didn't want to talk. But five minutes with Norman and she's singing like she's in a choir." She glanced at the robot. "What did you do? Or say to her?"

Norman finished nibbling on a radish. "I simply said, 'Would you like to sing with me?' When she was hesitant, I told her to follow my lead. All children enjoy singing. Once we got started, it was easy."

"Still, it's pretty amazing," Mom said, "a robot doing what several humans were unable to accomplish. Good work, um, Norman."

"Thank you, Maman," Norman said. For once Mom didn't turn purple when hc said this.

Dad was chewing and thinking.

"I can't say I understand it, but Norman appears to be going far beyond his programming," he said. "Norman is learning, and growing as a . . . person. If it wasn't happening before my eyes, I wouldn't believe it. But it truly seems he is absorbing cues from others, interpreting those cues, and learning from them as a way of humanizing himself." He nodded appreciatively. "Wow!"

"*Merci*, Papa," Norman said, apparently not knowing that a piece of radish was stuck between his porcelain teeth. *Gross!* "But I am certain that everything that happens with me is due to your advanced coding. Any other explanation would be illogical."

Mom smiled. "Norman is starting to sound just like you," she said to Dad.

"He's a real chip off the old block," Dad said, with an insane grin. "Get it, as in a microchip? Never mind!"

Pretty funny, for my dad. He doesn't have the best sense of humor.

"I've been thinking," Mom said. "Well . . . perhaps Norman can stay with us longer than a month. You know, for the sake of science. Why don't we get through the holidays and then decide what we want to do. Play it by ear." She turned toward the robot and slightly nodded at him.

Boy oh boy, was I glad that I dragged Norman along to the Community Help Center—it totally changed Mom's view of him. Go me! But I also thought that her change of heart had nothing to do with "science." Could Norman be growing on her? I wondered.

"Thank you for the extension, Maman," Norman said, after swallowing a chunk of something. "But what will happen to me when my time here is finished?"

I realized that no one had told Norman about the plan to eventually scrap him and Jean-Pierre Jr. and build more advanced robots.

"Uh, well," Dad said, avoiding Norman's eyes. "At some point we will travel to France so you can meet your uncle and brother." Yeah, meet them at a scrap yard!

"Wonderful," Norman said, dabbing at his mouth with a napkin. "I do wish to meet Jean-Pierre Junior and my uncle." But he was looking kind of nervous. Was it possible that he could tell when we were lying? Freaky thought, but it could be true.

Okay, I know you're wondering how Norman is able to eat, and what happens to the food, so let me explain. Norman chews his food just like you and I do, but when the level reaches a certain amount, a suction tube opens in his throat and directs the chewed food to a storage container in his butt.

That's right, his butt!

As it turns out, Norman's butt pulls out like a drawer so it can be easily emptied and cleaned. My brother has a removable butt!

But listen closely: I am never *ever* going to be the guy who empties and cleans Norman's butt. Not once! Grossness has its limits.

So now you know what happens to the food Norman eats. But maybe you wish you didn't? Too late!

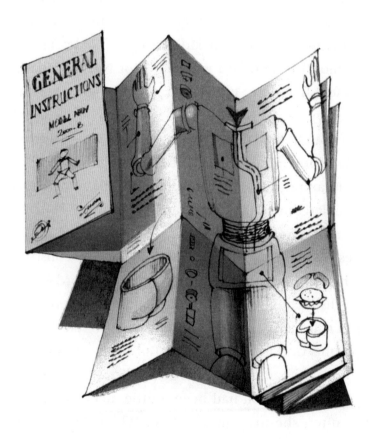

30.

For about a week nothing very exciting happened. Norman continued to excel at school, and I continued to feel like the brilliant kid's "average" older brother. But most of the time I was happy for Norman that he had found a way to be popular and have lots of friends. Good for him.

Though that one time in science class, Norman *really* annoyed me. Mr. Chambers sprang a surprise test on us, and during the entire time for the test Norman mumbled things like, "Four possible answers? There are at least twelve," and something about how true or false questions "are an outdated culturally relative construct." Huh? I sat next to him, so I heard every word—it was very distracting. When Mr. Chambers said that time was up, I still had four questions left unanswered. I ended up with a C. Norman got an A+. But so it goes when your brother is a battery-powered genius.

At home, Mom had been a little nicer to Norman, but often she just ignored him. When they did talk, which was rare, it was usually just a few words apiece. But Norman seemed to be handling Mom's cool approach a bit better. He was no longer talking to me about it, anyway.

And Dad was working on a program to keep Norman from slipping into hyper robot mode without approval from a family member. I began to wonder if my dad and uncle had invented the robots just so they'd have a ton of stuff to work on. It seemed like Dad was almost always in the lab, working on Norman or on his coding.

And Annie was hounding both Norman and me, confessing her undying love for us. Hey, at least I had someone to share the burden with.

So I guess—Wait! There was one weird thing that happened that week, either on Monday or Tuesday. While Norman, Annie, and I were waiting for the city bus to take us to school, I peered across the street and saw that the Edward building had a new doorman. For as long as I could remember, it had always been an older guy wearing a dark gray uniform. But this guy was younger and was wearing a maroon and gold uniform that looked like it would be more popular with band directors than doormen.

So the Edward got a new doorman. *Big deal,* I told myself. But just as I was about to turn my eyes away, the doorman started doing a little dance, a few leg kicks to the left and then to the right, like he was planning to audition for a Broadway musical and was practicing his moves.

Now I've seen everything!

Then it got even weirder. While I was watching the doorman dance, a man came speed-walking up the sidewalk, wearing a blue-and-white bodysuit that looked futuristic—and totally goofy!—and slipped between Norman and me. He stopped to check his watch, touched Norman's shoulder, and speed-walked away. No way! This is New York City. Strangers DO NOT touch strangers here. Even if they are on fire and need someone to call 911.

A dancing doorman. A touch-happy speed-walker in a funky outfit. I found myself suddenly full of that oogly, stomachache-y feeling that things were not what they appeared to be, that something else was going on just below the surface. And, as it turned out, I was right. But we're not to that part of the story yet, so hold your horses, buddy!

(In the meantime, I have some advice: Always trust your oogly feelings. Oogles. They *know* stuff.)

Before I could even try to wrap my head around what had just happened, the bus pulled up, and Norman, Annie, and I had to get on.

Nothing to worry about, I told myself as my brother and I settled into our seat. Doormen quit their jobs every day, and new doormen are hired to replace them.

And the speed-walker was probably from out of town, a resident of one of those touchy-feely states like Ohio or Kansas, and was not aware of our strict no-touching policy.

But as the bus pulled out, I glanced back at the Edward. The old doorman, the one with a gray uniform, was back on the job. The dancing guy with the flashy uniform was nowhere in sight. *That's it,* I told myself, *I'm officially losing it.*

Let's jump forward to that Wednesday.

When I woke up before dawn, I saw that Norman was not in his box.

Or the closet.

Or my toy chest.

So I stumbled out of my room and checked the living room, no Norman, then I went into the kitchen where I saw Norman, wearing only his antistatic undies and one sock, lying on the kitchen table and saying, "*Le lapin a mangé mes pommes de terre.* The rabbit ate my potatoes." He said that silly sentence twice more before realizing I was in the room. "*Bonjour,* Luke," he said, looking at me with one eye. "Did you enjoy the turnip delight that Uncle Wilbur prepared for you?"

"My name is Matt," I said. Not brilliant, but part of my brain was still sleeping. Even the sun wasn't up yet. Also, I had no idea what "turnip delight" was. "Turnip" and "delight" should never be in the same sentence. And I don't have an uncle named Wilbur.

Then Norman's right arm started shaking, and his eye, the one that wasn't looking at me, blinked so rapidly I couldn't count the blinks. "Misaligned frog alert!" he said. "Gentlemen, arm your tornadoes!"

It was one of those things that was two parts funny and three parts scary, like the day our neighbor, Mr. Muldoon, lost control of his car near our building and crashed into a fire hydrant. No one was hurt, but the freaked-out look on Mr. Muldoon's face as he tried to get control of his car . . . I nearly laughed myself out of my pants, as Dad sometimes said.

Anyway, I wasn't sure what to do about Norman. I was thinking about waking up Dad, but no need, he was shuffling into the kitchen, running a hand through his crazy hair.

"What are you guys doing up this early?" he asked. "Juvenile high jinks with a side order of hoopla?" I told you that my dad sometimes talks funny.

Norman sat up and said, "*Bonjour*, Maman. It's Tuesday, so please don't iron the cold cuts. Orange cake!"

There were at least three problems with those sentences. First, Dad was a *papa*, not a *maman*. Second, it was Wednesday, not Tuesday. Third, only a loon would iron cold cuts. But the orange cake sounded tasty.

"I wonder if Norman caught a virus during his latest

software update," Dad said, scratching at his chest, "though theoretically that should not be possible, since it's a closed-loop system." He stepped closer to the robot. "Norman, run a self-diagnostic of your hardware and software."

Norman smiled in the broken way, the left side of his mouth rising up and the right side doing nothing. *"Je suis désolé, humain,"* he said. "I'm sorry, human. Self-diagnostics disabled. Show tunes enabled."

The robot then jumped up and began singing "Oh, What a Beautiful Morning," right there on the kitchen table. But before I could applaud, or join in, my dad grabbed Norman and pressed his power button until he went dead. Dad's forehead was wrinkled with worry.

"We'll be in the lab until further notice," he said grimly, carrying the machine toward the door. "Please do not disturb us."

Get well, Norman, I thought with all my thinking power. At five in the morning that was about six watts.

I couldn't get back to sleep due to worrying about Norman, so I watched some TV, even though there was nothing good on, just reruns of old shows like *Frasier* and *Saved by the Bell.* Of course, there was always the *Wake Up, America* show with Fig Ferrell and the gang. . . . Not!

When my mom appeared with a yawn, we went into the kitchen so she could fix breakfast for us, me shrugging when she asked why the tablecloth was rumpled and out of place. A shrug doesn't count as a lie. It's just moving your shoulders.

We ate scrambled free-range eggs and Corn Flakes in organic milk. I was in a race to finish the cornflakes before they turned mushy, but Mom said, "Slow down, Dale Earnhardt Junior," so I slowed down a little.

I then told Mom that Norman might have a virus, and that's how come he and Dad were in the lab. She didn't look too concerned. But then she gazed at me and soaked up some of my worry, like she was willing to be worried about Norman since I was.

"Your father is a genius," she said. "If there's a problem, he'll fix it. Norman will be fine."

"I know," I said, spooning cornflake mush around in the bowl and wondering when science will come up with a mush-free cornflake. Are they even working on it?

That was when goopy sadness invaded. What would happen to Norman if Dad couldn't fix him? I wondered. Would he end up on a junk pile somewhere, eleven months ahead of schedule?

I can't explain it, but I started to cry. Right into my cornflakes! I had become as mushy as my cereal. Jeez.

Mom ran a hand through my hair and patted it as a way of saying that Norman was going to be okay. Why do adults do that, pat your hair when they know you are blue? Your hair is never where it hurts.

31.

My dad stayed home from work so he could repair Norman. I tried to get out of going to school so I could help, but that didn't fly.

It was a big chore just to get to homeroom. Nearly every kid I ran into wanted to know where Norman was. "Where's your cool brother from France?"—that kind of thing. Some of the kids like Annie Bananas and Jenny Huffleman were even being pushy about it, like I must be hiding Norman from them.

That was when Principal Jackson saved me. He pushed through the crowd of kids, telling them to get to class. The kids fled. But there was still Principal J. to deal with.

"You and I need to have a talk, Mr. Rambeau," he said in his super-serious voice. Come to think of it, that might be the only voice he has.

On the way to the office I tried to think of stupid things I'd done lately to draw Principal J.'s interest, like that day in September when I stumbled around like a zombie all morning because Jeter had dared me to. No reason to play Truth or Dare if you're not willing to do the dares. My mistake? Telling Kayla Rafferty that I wanted to *eat her brain*! She tattled. I nearly got a detention.

In the office, Principal Jackson leaned back in his chair and tapped his fingers against each other. If I did that, I'd probably be told to sit up straight and stop playing with my hands.

"Your brother is not like the rest of our students, is he?" Principal Jackson said carefully. "I mean, it's almost like night and day. Am I the only one seeing how different he is?"

I froze. This could be bad. *Very* bad. If Principal Jackson went public with the fact that Norman was a robot, and reporters invaded our lives, my dad might end the experiment early and scrap Norman, to keep Mom from freaking out. The same thing could happen in France, if word got out that there were two robots. I could lose my robot brother and my robot cousin, all due to Principal J. spilling the beans.

But maybe there was a way to stop him, I thought. Like what if I offered to wash his car once a week, or something like that, in return for silence? I didn't think he'd take a cash bribe, since he's a principal. Besides, I'm a kid. I never have much cash.

"How did you figure out that Norman is . . . different?"

I asked, thinking that my dad would want to know that information for his research.

"Well, the early reports I'm getting from faculty suggest that Norman is gifted—perhaps even a genius—and also a skilled gymnast." He leaned forward and clasped his hands together. "You know what this could mean for our school, don't you?"

I shook my head while thinking, *Phew, what a relief!* The Norman-is-a-robot beans had *not* been spilled. Not yet, anyway.

"It could mean we'll finally win first prize at the state science fair in January"—Principal Jackson's voice was getting weirdly high-pitched and excited, I must point out—"and the biggest trophy at the Math Olympics in April. Heck, maybe Norman will even win the National Spelling Bee for us. So what this means, Mr. Rambeau, is that with your brother's help West Side Middle School may finally get the recognition it deserves!"

Fascinating, in a *yawn yawn yawn* kind of way. Principal Jackson was completely clueless that Norman was a robot. Yay!

As I was waiting for a "Dismissed," Principal J. leaned over the desk, like he wanted to take me into his confidence. I was seeing his nose hairs. It was way too early in the day for nose hairs.

"But here's the thing," he told me. "If word of Norman's talents spreads beyond the walls of this building, no doubt your brother will be transferred to one of the gifted schools. We need him here more than they need him there, so I'd like to put that off for as long as possible."

Thinking that Principal J. was about to ask for a favor, I slouched, figuring I could get away with it.

"So I'm wondering if you might ask Norman to turn it down a notch," he asked, "not give everyone the idea that he's the next Einstein or a future Olympian. Could you do that for me, Matt?"

Why not—I had also been hoping my brother would turn it down a notch. "I'll talk to Norman as soon as he's feeling better," I said.

"He's not well?"

"He might have caught a virus."

"Lots of nasty things are going around this time of year," Principal Jackson said. "I'm sure he'll be fine in a few days."

Principal J. then signed a pass so I wouldn't get in trouble for being late to homeroom. "There is one more thing," he said, before I could grab the pass. "Stop slouching! Slouchers never go far in life." You know, he might have been right. Think of presidents, famous athletes, and movie stars. You almost never see them slouching.

So I straightened up, stood up, and left for homeroom. On the way there I passed the janitor, pushing a mop bucket down the hall. "Hey there, Oscar," I said, but then I realized that this person was not Oscar. Instead it was a younger guy with a beard and mustache, but the weird part was that the mustache and beard were different shades of brown, and neither of them matched the color of the hair on his head.

He looked at me, frowned, and turned away. Thanks for the love, new guy!

Hmm. I thought that I had seen this dude before, but where? Not the comic book shop . . . Not the cleaner's . . . Not the bagel bakery . . . Maybe I'd remember later, I told myself, if I could remember to remember.

I turned down a hallway, but stopped when I thought I heard the janitor talking to someone. I inched along the lockers until I could see him again. He was talking on a cell phone, which we students aren't allowed to do. Man, grown-ups. They get to have all the fun.

"Clean out your ears, idiot," he said to someone. "I said it looks like he's not here, so maybe it worked. But we really need to stop wasting time and get this job over with. The sooner the better, so we can return home and get on with our lives." Whatever the other person said back to him, the janitor didn't like it. He hissed, snapped the phone shut, and slipped it into a pocket. He then started pushing the mop bucket toward the main doors like he was planning to mop outside. Innovative!

Well, that was strange, but I'd have to think about it later: I was running late for class.

Just as I was nearing homeroom I saw Oscar, the normal janitor, cleaning a water fountain. "We have a second janitor now?" I said, trying to be friendly.

Oscar glared at me in a hurt kind of way. "A second janitor?" he said. "Don't tease me like that, young man. A second janitor to share the workload has been a dream of mine for twenty-three years." He sighed and went back to work. Sorry, Oscar.

As soon as I opened the door to homeroom . . .

"Hi, Norman!" a few kids said, but then they got all frowny and disappointed when they saw that it was only me.

Yep, just me. Nothing to get excited about, kids.

52.

Back home. Norman was in pieces on the worktable in the lab. Dad was hovering over him, tightening tiny screws near a hipbone. It was freaky seeing my brother's head removed, wires dangling out of the neck opening. It was almost like he was . . . dead.

"How's Norman doing?" I asked, trying to not look at the robot's head, but my stupid eyes kept going back there.

"Not so great," Dad said. "Norman and his cousin have been infected with a computer worm that wreaked havoc on their core files. I believe we stopped it from causing any more harm, so now it's a matter of fixing the damage and restoring lost data."

On a video screen on the computer, I watched my uncle make similar repairs to Jean-Pierre Jr. Two headless kid-bots! My stomach was getting a little queasied out. "Is Norman going to be okay?"

Dad shrugged. "Time will tell. But even if we can get him up and running, it may take a while before he's his old self again. The worm tore through his files like a missile with teeth."

I looked at helpless Norman and felt awful about every bad or selfish thought I'd ever had about him. So what if he was more popular or smarter than I was? I just wanted him to be okay.

When the screws were tightened, my dad and uncle had a video chat. Parts of it were in French, but from the English parts and from knowing more French since Norman showed up, I could figure out some of it. Basically, my dad and uncle were baffled at how a worm was able to bust through firewalls and into encrypted files, especially since the software programming the robots existed only on Dad's and my uncle's computers.

"It's almost like this was an inside job," Dad said, going back to English. "But only a half-dozen people know about Norman and Jean-Pierre Junior, and we trust all of them, right?"

My uncle suddenly looked pale. "I would trust my two assistants with my life," he affirmed.

Dad gave him a look. "And what about Véronique?"

Uncle Jean-Pierre scratched at his face and seemed kind of embarrassed.

"Jean-Pierre?" Dad prodded. "Is there anything you want to tell me?"

"Véronique left me two days ago," my uncle finally said. "She said she could not be with a man who cares more about computers and robots than he does his girlfriend. It was quite a surprise. I thought . . . Well, I stupidly believed that she was the one."

Dad appeared sympathetic for a moment, but then switched to a look of grave concern. "I hate to ask . . . but . . . could she have planted the worm? Would she do that, sabotage our work?"

My uncle shook his head fiercely, but even while he was doing that I could see a big pile of doubt creep into his face. "She's more of a materials person than a software person, so she would have needed outside help launching a worm," he said. After a deep sigh, he added, "Véronique is mad at me for not paying attention to her, but I can't imagine her wanting to harm the robots. She worked on them for years, just like we did."

"Can you find her, see what she knows?" Dad asked. "If she has been talking to the wrong people . . ." His voice got really quiet.

My uncle pointed behind Dad, at me, I think. I guess they didn't want to talk about that subject with me in the room. Sometimes it rots being a kid.

Uncle Jean-Pierre cut the link after saying he needed food and a café au lait. And I wondered if my dad had eaten anything all day. He had done that before, worked in his lab all day, skipping lunch and dinner.

Dad went back to work on the robot.

"Can I help with Norman?" I asked. "Like hand you a screwdriver or something?"

"Oh, sure," Dad said, smiling. He pointed to a screwdriver. I picked it up and handed it to him, and he started removing the casing around Norman's hard drives and RAM modules. It was almost like we were in an operating room, and I was the guy in charge of handing the surgeon the correct scalpel, or screwdriver. It was a big job.

"How's Norman doing?" Mom asked when I returned to the apartment. She was in the kitchen, searching through the fridge, trying to find something to fix for dinner.

"The next twenty-four hours will be crucial," I said, words I might have heard on one of those hospital TV shows, instead of something Dad said. But it sounded right.

"Matt, you know your dad—he can fix anything computerized," Mom said. "Norman is in the best hands possible." This time she looked truly concerned for the robot. She didn't have to borrow any concern from me.

And what she said was totally true. As far as robot surgery goes, my dad was probably the top guy in all of New York City. Maybe in all of the Western Hemisphere! This made me feel better about Norman's chances.

Much to my surprise, Mom pulled a frozen blueberry pie from the freezer. "Is this okay?" she asked. "We should probably eat it up before freezer burn has its evil way."

Pie for dinner? I thought I could only dream of living

in that world! I nodded quickly like a goof before Mom changed her mind.

She slipped the pie into the oven, and then we watched some TV in the living room. It was still prime kid-TV time, so I was in charge of the remote. Sometimes when I'm watching cartoons with Mom or Dad they can get kind of critical of the shows—"A talking sponge? Really?"—but that day Mom and I were quietly hanging out together like two friends watching cartoons. I liked that way loads better.

I glanced at Mom—she had fallen asleep, I think. Or at least her eyes were closed. Must have had a tough day at work. Oh well, so it wasn't the perfect mom and son bonding moment. Ninety-five percent perfect was good enough for me.

After the pie cooled down it was time for dinner. Of course Mom and I weren't having only blueberry pie, that would have been unhealthy. The side dish was a big scoop of organic vanilla ice cream. MADE WITH THE HELP OF HAPPY COWS, said the carton.

"Dive in," Mom said, smiling at me, then jabbing a fork into her slice of pie. So I dove in, feeling pretty lucky that I had parents who more often than not knew exactly what I needed, even when I didn't always know what I needed. Like pie for dinner!

Another thing I love? Warm blueberry pie served with a side of vanilla ice cream. For dinner!

34.

It took Dad working all night and into the morning to get Norman back together again and powered up. Going inside the lab to check on my brother, I saw him sitting on the worktable, gazing into space. Dad, his eyes buggy from no sleep, was at the computer, typing code. He had decided that Norman wouldn't be going to school that day. Lots of files to check.

I tried to cheer up Norman.

"Good morning!" I said to him. "You're looking very . . . together."

It took Norman maybe five seconds to look at me.

"*Bonjour. Comment allez-vous?*" he said.

"Um, I'm okay. You know who I am, right?"

"*Oui.* You are . . . processing . . . processing . . . Matthew Rambeau Junior, offspring of my cocreator, Matthew Rambeau Senior."

I'd never thought of myself as an "offspring" before. Sounded kind of insectlike.

"Right," I said to Norman encouragingly, though I

wasn't feeling too encouraged. "And you know that I'm your brother?" I asked him.

Norman nodded. I decided to give the kid a hug, hoping it would help speed up his recovery.

"*Excuse-moi*, Matthew," Norman said, during the hug. "But I believe you are blocking my main air vent."

Argh! This was too freaky weird. Norman was more robot-y than Norman-y. He was even more robot-y than when he first came out of the crate! I glanced at Dad. He scratched his scalp. "There's more coding to fix," he said, "but I'll have to do it later. Missing another day of work wouldn't be fair to my students."

So Dad left for his college, Mom left for the Community Help Center, and I went to school. But before any of that happened, Dad turned Norman off, concerned he might tear up the apartment or wander off. The pre-worm Norman would never have even considered vandalizing out apartment, but this one . . .

I wanted the real Norman back!

55.

On the bus and at school lots of kids and some teachers asked how Norman was doing, but not as many as the day before. Annie and Jeter were still worried about my brother, but when I saw Jenny Huffleman in computer lab she didn't ask a thing, or even look my way. True love doesn't last long in the sixth grade, I guess. Or maybe Norman Mania was already wearing off.

So school felt a little more pre-Norman normal, but . . . that was a bad thing. I liked it much better when he was there. For one, you never know what to expect from that kid. Like the time he barrel-rolled down the entire length of the main hallway for no known reason, kids and teachers having to jump out of the way. Freaky, but fresh! Maybe no other kid anywhere had done that, ever.

Normanless and seriously bummed, I just wanted the school day to end. But wouldn't you know it, all the clocks were stuck on *slowwwwwww.* . . .

School eventually ended, and I was hanging out

again with Norman. I thought that doing some typical brother stuff might help pull him out of his robot funk, so we went to the skate park a few blocks from our building, where I was planning to teach him how to skateboard. We were both wearing elbow pads and knee pads and a helmet—a requirement if you want to skate at a city park. I felt skater-dude cool and kid-with-pads uncool at the same time.

Fortunately, we were by ourselves—except for a skinny parks department worker sitting on a bench and reading a book—and that might have been due to the weather: It had gotten kind of chilly and windy, so Norman and I had put on jackets before leaving. I actually had never given thought to whether Norman could get hot or cold. So I asked him.

"Heat is a concern to all computers, so I have heat sensors throughout my shell," he said, "and I am programmed to shut down if temperatures reach a critical level. Cold is much less of a concern, though my operations may slow considerably if exposed to subzero temperatures for a considerable length of time."

Okay then!

I dropped my board to the concrete and demonstrated some of my best boarding for Norman, rolling up and down two ramps—it's kind of a lame-o park, having just three ramps and two rails—but when I was finished he looked at me like he was completely baffled.

"*Pardonne-moi,*" Norman said, "but I am not sure I understand the purpose of this sport. Is all that is required of me is to ride up the ramp to my left, roll down it, then ride up the ramp to my right, repeating the procedure?"

"That's most of it," I said. "But feel free to bust some moves, if you like: jumps, turns, bending low and grabbing the board. . . ." Moves are my weak point. I need more moves.

"And that is how I will score points, by 'busting some moves'?"

"Nope, no points are involved, at least at this level," I said. "We're doing it just for fun."

Norman shook his head, like fun was an alien concept. I handed him my board. "Show me what you got, Frenchy," I said.

The robot adjusted his helmet, chomped his mouth a few times—don't ask me why, I was clueless—set the board down, stepped his right foot on it, and began kicking off the concrete with his left foot. Good, but he was going way too fast.

"Slow down!" I warned, too late—Norman was really zipping up the ramp. I closed one eye, fearing that a broken bot catastrophe was looming as Norman and the board went flying off the ramp, maybe fifteen feet into the air, then he crouched and grabbed hold of the board, turned upside down and right side up—*eeeeeee!!!*—and landed on the ramp with the board, rolled smoothly down it, and parked the board at my feet.

Perfect, but also kind of show-offy. But at least that meant that one part of Norman was back to normal. The show-off part.

"How was that, Matt?" he asked, looking a little too pleased with himself. "Acceptable?"

"Not too bad for a first-timer," I said, putting on a smile. But to be honest, I wasn't completely happy on the inside, all of my seeing-Norman-in-pieces-and-willing-to-do-anything-to-put-him-back-together good-will instantly evaporating. I was hoping there was one thing, like boarding, that I was better at than Norman. Just one thing! That was all I needed.

"Thank you," the robot said flatly. "I simply compensated for gravity and air resistance and adjusted my trajectory and forward movement appropriately. Though I will confess to enjoying the sensation of being airborne, of having, albeit ever so briefly, shaken off gravity's insistent grip."

Whatever!

As I was about to jump on my board and work on some moves, I saw Annie Bananas, wearing pink elbow and knee pads and a purple helmet and carrying her skateboard, gallop up to us. Her board had a picture of a Disney cartoon princess on it. Big surprise, huh?

"Norman! Matt!" she said, waving her right arm

around like a spaz. "Your dad told me you'd be here!"

Thanks, Dad.

"Uh, hey, Bananas," I barely said.

Annie moved closer to Norman. "How are you feeling?" she asked. "All better?"

The robot blinked a few times. *"Excusez-moi, petite fille, mais je ne crois pas que je vous connais."*

"What did he say?" Annie asked me.

"Please translate what you just said," I told my brother.

"Entschuldigen Sie mich, kleines Mädchen, aber ich glaube nicht daß, ich Sie kenne," Norman said.

"I meant in English!" I said.

The robot seemed to freeze for a moment, then said, "I said, 'Excuse me, little girl, but I don't believe I know you.'"

Annie's mouth dropped open. If you were there, you would have seen her teeth and fat tongue, and the weird lizardy webbing under her tongue. Good thing for you you weren't there.

"Of course you know me," she cried. "I'm Annie! We've seen each other a zillion times. We were practically boyfriend and girlfriend until Matt told you some lies about me." She aimed her best snarl at me.

"Processing . . . Processing . . ." Norman said. "No, I do not have any Annie files as it pertains to you. *Annie* the popular musical about the adventures of an orphan girl and her stray dog, yes. *Annie Hall,* a movie by the

172

adorably quirky Woody Allen, yes. Annie you, no. Apologies."

Annie's mouth dropped back open. Please stop doing that!

"Norman isn't all better yet from the virus," I told her. "He's still a little . . . foggy."

"Excuse me, Matt," Norman said, "but I believe that Papa determined it was a worm, not a virus, a troubling variant of the Doomsday Sandwich worm that destroyed many of my—"

"Norman?" I interrupted. "I don't think Annie needs to know the dirty details."

Annie's face was scrunched. "Norman had worms? Gross! I definitely do not need to know the details." She shrugged, set her board down, and wheeled it across the concrete and up one of the ramps. Annie is actually a pretty good skater. That's the *only* cool thing about her.

While she was rolling down the ramp, a silver car with squeaky brakes—an Audi, I think—stopped at the curb near the skate park, then two men with long beards and wearing black coats and hats crawled out of it. My first thought was they were Orthodox Jews, but then I decided that they looked more Amish-like. Living in New York City, I've seen just about every kind of person in every kind of situation. A Hispanic lady pushing three cats in a stroller? Seen it! A white guy talking into his hand like it's a cell phone and saying, "Cheese? I did not order any cheese!"? Seen it! But I had never seen Amish people riding in a car. Shouldn't they have been in a horse and buggy?

One of the men grabbed a duffel bag from the car, and they started walking toward us. Hmm. They sure didn't look like skateboarders, unless they had boards in that bag. Handcrafted Amish boards with wooden wheels! That would have been sort of cool.

"Look at me, look at me!" Annie demanded as she did a one-eighty at the top of a ramp. But . . . something felt a little off. I shifted my eyes back to the two bearded guys, getting closer to us. Hah! One of the men's beards was peeling off. It was a fake! The other guy, the one carrying the duffel bag, noticed it too and got the attention of his friend, who stopped walking and frantically patted at his beard. Fakers! But why would anyone want to pass themselves off as Amish?

Wait a sec. . . .

Wait a freakin' sec! I knew those guys! The guy with the falling-off beard was the same guy who'd been mopping the floor at my school. And . . . hold on a minute, the dancing doorman at the Edward! And the mime! It all seemed to click together in my brain. And the other man . . . he had to be the speed-walker and the guy with the video camera, the day of the mime. But that must mean . . . Oh boy. A prickly feeling of being in serious danger came over me, but I needed to keep it together somehow. *What should I do?* I asked myself. Try to get the attention of the parks worker? Grab Norman's hand and run?

I glanced at Norman and Annie, and then at the men. They were just standing there, about fifteen feet away, like they were deciding their next move.

That was when three high school boys clutching boards and wearing mostly black—they all think they're the next Tony Hawk—appeared at the park, one of the boys giving me a *Take a seat, son, and watch some pros show you how to skate* kind of look. Used to it! Then one of the other boys—let's call him Ringo, since he had like ten rings in his nose and ears—spotted the bearded men. "Amish boarders?" he said. "No way!" He pulled out a phone like he was planning to snap a picture, but the men were scurrying to their car and getting back in. The driver started it and they drove off, speeding down the street.

Safe for now, I thought, not knowing that I'd soon see these two guys again. But more on that later. You know the drill. It's not yet later.

I needed to tell Dad about the strange men. But I didn't want to alarm Norman or Annie, so I took in a huge breath and let it out slowly, the way my mom does when she needs to de-stress.

Meanwhile, Norman was giving Annie and the high school kids a lesson in the physics of skateboarding. "The energy created by skating up the ramp is, as you probably already know, converted into kinetic energy on the way down," he said, all junior Einstein–like. "The kinetic energy you gain is then converted back into potential energy as you move up the next ramp. Of course, let us not forget that the Newtonian law of equal and opposite reactions comes into play whenever you . . ."

That was where Norman lost me. Or a little ways back.

When the robot finished his rant, the older boys gave each other confused looks, then started skating. And Annie crossed her arms and narrowed her eyes and said to Norman and me, "Something funny is going on here. Kids don't talk that way, what Norman just said. And kids don't forget meeting other kids and being kissed by them. What are you guys up to? I'm going to get to the bottom of this if it turns me blue!"

That would have been a riot, seeing Annie turn blue, but I could barely think about that—I couldn't get those two men out of my head. Norman and I better go home, I decided. So I grabbed my board and told Annie that it was time for my brother and me to go eat dinner. She suddenly looked all flumpy and bummed out. Sorry!

Naturally, Annie followed us home, wiggling in between Norman and me. As we neared our building, a chilly wind whipped at us, then a few snowflakes started to fall. Norman watched the snowflakes, then totally wigged out and tore off his jacket. "We are under attack from the sky!" he said. "Run, Matt and Miss Annie!" He dashed toward the front door, swishing his arms around to fight off the killer snowflakes.

An attack from the sky? Genius! Now that was the Norman I liked hanging with, the total nutball. Even though Annie was still within smelling distance, I started to feel a little bit better.

36.

While Dad was running diagnostic tests on Norman, the robot in suspended animation mode, I told him the easy thing first, that Norman was frightened of snow.

"How strange," he said, wrinkling his face. "I was sure we wrote some data about snow and precipitation into Norman's code. The worm must have gobbled it up."

Norman was hooked up by HDMI cable to a computer monitor. I watched long strings of code scroll across the screen and had a thought. Change one letter or number or symbol, and you change Norman. That was also true with people. Change an X or a Y chromosome or a this or a that and you have a completely different person.

That thought weirded me out. One little chromosome switcheroo and I could have been born a girl. A girl!

Once I pulled myself together . . .

"So the worm was on purpose?" I asked my dad while he was studying Norman's coding. "Someone wanted to hurt Norman and Jean-Pierre Junior?"

Dad nodded, his eyes glued to the monitor. "Whenever there is something new and great, there will always be a few people trying to destroy it or stop it. They are afraid of change, I guess." He tapped at a few keys. "But if we were all afraid of change to the point that fear crippled us, we'd still be fish swimming in an unchangeable sea."

Well, that made sense. Smart guy, my dad.

He disconnected Norman from the monitor and immediately put him in sleep mode. "Norman should rest for a while. He's had a rough couple days."

"But he's okay now? No more worm?"

"From a programming and structural standpoint, yes, Norman is perfectly fine," Dad said. "But the worm caused profound changes. When Norman first arrived, I think he substantially thought of himself as a boy. But now it's as if he knows he's a robot and is behaving accordingly. Your uncle is reporting a similar experience with Jean-Pierre Junior—it's like the worm took away part of his personality. It might take considerable effort to bring back the boy in Norman."

I nodded, accessed my courage genes, and told Dad the more difficult thing, about the two strange men showing up at the bus stop, at my school, and at the skate park. The words came out really fast.

Worry lines erupted on Dad's forehead. "Are you sure it's been the same men, each time?"

"It's the same guys," I said, 99.999 percent sure. "But they were wearing uniforms and disguises, so it took me a while to figure it out. Sorry."

"You did fine," my dad said, his brain cranking away. Suddenly his eyes went wide. "Tell me, did either of the men touch Norman? Were they ever that close?"

"Why?"

"Because your uncle and I believe we have figured out how the worm was able to do so much damage," he said in a calmer, more fatherly voice. "Before launching the worm attack on Norman and Jean-Pierre Junior, whoever did this sent in thousands of nanobots on one mission, to tear through firewalls before destroying themselves. But everything leaves behind tracings, if you know where to look. Your uncle and I found a few broken nanobots inside Norman and Jean-Pierre Junior that failed to do their job."

Nanobots? "Tiny robots?" I asked my dad.

"That's right," he said. "They are too small to be seen by the naked eye. But you can't deliver nanobots by computer; you have to have a physical entry point. So that's why it's important to know if either of the men touched Norman."

I replayed my encounters with the creepy guys. "The speed-walker! When he walked by us he touched Norman on the shoulder!"

Dad did a quick inspection of Norman, then peeled

off a nearly invisible patch about the size of a small Band-Aid, near Norman's neck. He examined it, then held it closer to me so I could take a look.

"Not sure how I missed this earlier—the color is astonishingly similar to Norman's skin tone—but they used a skin patch to deliver the nanobots. I can't believe it!" he said. "This is CIA-level stuff. I thought we were still years away from this kind of microtechnology. Incredible!"

I wasn't sure what to say. Nanobots. Skin patches. Computer worms. It was a little overwhelming.

"I don't suppose you got a license plate number on their car?" Dad asked. "You know, the one belonging to the, for lack of a better word, spies?"

I shook my head no.

He frowned. "If you see the car again, try to get the plate number," he said. "For now, until we figure out what's going on, I'm going to change my work schedule so I can drive you and Norman to and from school." His voice turned grave. "If their mission was to destroy the robots, by now they surely know . . . Let's just do everything we can to stay safe."

I went from medium scared to very scared. But I definitely wasn't flipping out!

Dad said he didn't want to be rude, but he needed to have a private chat with Jean-Pierre. I glanced at sleeping Norman, wondered if robots dream when they are in sleep mode, and started to leave.

"Sport?" Dad said. "Let's not say anything to your mother about the two men just yet, okay? It might disrupt . . . Well, let's wait for the right time."

I nodded, thinking that was a good plan. As soon as Mom heard the word "spies," she'd send Norman away on the next FedEx flight to France. Of course, when she did find out what had been going on it would be twice as bad for Dad and me for keeping the secret. But we weren't there yet.

I was about to leave the lab when I had a thought. As a kid I was used to being sent out of the room so adults could have a serious discussion, but this time . . . Well, if Dad and Uncle Jean-Pierre were talking about important stuff involving my brother, I thought I had a right to know. So I turned toward my dad just as he was clicking on the video chat icon.

"Um, can I stay just this once?" I asked. "Since it's about Norman, I . . . Well, I'd really like to stay."

Dad gave me a long look, then nodded. I quickly took a seat next to him at the computer. Wow! It was like I had been welcomed into a club that I thought I was years away from joining.

When Uncle Jean-Pierre came online he gave me a smile. I returned it, trying to look serious and adultlike, but for some reason I felt like giggling. Jeez—what the heck is wrong with me? (If your answer is "You're a total Froot Loop, Matt," you just might be right.)

"Big news," Dad said to his brother—in English, for my benefit. "I've discovered, with Matt's help, how they delivered the nanobots—by skin patch. I found this patch on Norman's shoulder." He held the patch up to the camera. "Didn't you tell me that Jean-Pierre Junior had an encounter with a stranger a day or two before the worm was launched?"

"Yes, with a tourist asking for directions to the Eiffel Tower," my uncle said, after a short delay.

"Check Jean-Pierre Junior from top to tail—no doubt you'll find a similar patch," Dad told him. "It seems to have been a highly efficient delivery method. And it means that whoever we are dealing with has excellent resources."

Uncle Jean-Pierre rubbed his face with both hands, like he was trying to smooth it out. My dad hesitated for a moment, then said, "I trust that you haven't seen Véronique?"

"No," my uncle said, giving his face one last rub. "When I went to her apartment to confront her about the worm, it was completely empty, cleared out. She's gone! No forwarding address, and none of the neighbors knew where she had moved to." He looked to be in so much pain I wanted to give him a big hug. But remote hugging hasn't been invented yet.

"That definitely makes her suspect number one, in my mind," my dad said. "But obviously she had helpers, here and in France. Who *are* these people?"

Uncle Jean-Pierre threw his arms up in a shrug. Wanting to say something, I raised my hand, then quickly dropped it. This wasn't school! "Why would Véronique want to harm the robots?" I asked. To me, planting a worm in Norman and Jean-Pierre Jr. would be like poisoning two real kids. Who could do such a thing?

Plus, Véronique had always been nice to me whenever I'd seen her on chat. Not once did I think she was evil. Could Dad and Uncle Jean-Pierre be wrong about her?

My uncle was shaking his head miserably, so I looked to my dad for answers, but he looked as baffled as Jean-Pierre. So I cranked up my brain, and, once it warmed up, I spat out a few thoughts of my own.

Like that maybe people and robots aren't that much different. Robot files can be corrupted by things like worms and viruses, and people files by things like . . . greed. And jealousy. And . . . the wish for revenge, too. With Véronique, I didn't know why she might want to hurt the robots—if she was responsible—but could the answer simply be this: bad files?

While I was congratulating my brain for a rare burst of smartness, Dad let out a sigh, then told his brother that two men wearing disguises had been spying on Norman and me, and possibly they were the same men responsible for the nanobots and the computer worm.

"I have also gotten the feeling lately that Jean-Pierre Junior and I are being watched," my uncle reported. "I thought I was being more paranoid than usual, but perhaps not. If we are being spied on, it's quite possible that they might soon be coming for the robots. *Un homme averti en vaut deux.*"

"Huh?" I said, building up worry about what my uncle had just said.

"Forewarned is forearmed," Dad translated, tightening up his face.

A silent moment followed that was so tense it almost seemed noisy. Then my uncle said he needed to end the chat so he could check the locks on his doors and windows. "If this goes bad on us and there are no other options, don't forget Norman's fail-safe code," he said.

"Lucien's birth date repeated twice—can't forget that," Dad said, with some sadness.

"Yes, I suppose you won't forget. . . ," Uncle Jean-Pierre said gently.

As they signed off, I wondered what the heck a fail-safe code was. For some reason I didn't feel I could ask my dad, like if he wanted me to know what it was I'd already know. A fail-safe code . . . It sounds like a bad thing, doesn't it?

During dinner—just me, Mom, and Dad, Norman was sleeping—Dad said that it was time for this family to "improve security measures." First, he told Mom that he was going to start driving Norman and me to and from school. Then he said that tomorrow morning he'd contact a security company about installing an alarm system and security cameras in our apartment and the lab, and that he was going to buy cell phones for Norman and me so we could all check in with each other when Norman and I were at school and Mom and Dad were at work.

While I was thinking, *Cool, I can call Jeter twenty times a day to talk about dumb stuff, or make barnyard noises,* Dad said the phones would be for "family talk" and emergency use only. I should have known there was a catch. With parents and cool stuff there's *always* a catch.

"Also," Dad said, glancing my way, "I'm not sure it's safe for you and Norman to play outside unsupervised. If you can't drag your mother or me outside with you, well, I'm afraid you'll have to stay inside, for now."

It looked like Norman and I wouldn't be playing outside much, at least Monday through Friday. My parents are not outdoors people during the week. But most Saturdays and Sundays they put on their "weekend warrior" outfits and morph into different people, seekers of sunshine and green spaces. It's pretty crazy.

"Do these new security measures have anything to do with Norman and his worm?" Mom asked, eyeing my father. "I'm not saying they don't make sense, it's just that they are rather sudden."

"In some ways, yes," Dad said, spooning pad kee mao (Thai food!) from a carton and onto his plate. "With Norman having been maliciously attacked—even if it was a cyber-attack—I realized that I needed to do more to protect my family."

Mom seemed to accept the explanation, which I think was one of those half-truths. Dad left out the parts about the spies, nanobots, and my uncle's missing girl-friend. I guess he was trying to keep Mom from blowing a sprocket. That's *always* a good idea.

I went back to trying to stack green beans from my serving of pad kee mao into a pyramid—not as easy as it sounds. According to the carryout menu they were organic beans, which meant no pesticides were used, which also meant that a lightning bug could have peed on them and gotten away with it. Something to think about next time you eat organic green beans.

37.

When it was time for bed, Norman slipped inside his box. Apparently, the worm hadn't chewed up his weird thing for boxes. I thought this could mean that more of *that* Norman, *our* Norman, was coming back.

"What am I?" the robot asked. "And why am I here?"

Argh! I'm twelve, too young to philosophize about the meaning of life. I haven't even figured out girls yet! Plus, it was late and I was tired. My eyelids *really* wanted to meet each other.

"You're Norman," I said. "That's who you are."

"But who exactly is 'Norman,' and why does he, or it, exist?"

The robot was going to pester me until I came up with something smart. With this brain that sometimes takes a while.

"Norman is my brother," I said. "As far as why he exists . . . um, let me think about that one." I'm still trying to figure out why *I* exist.

"Excuse-moi," Norman said. "While it is pleasant to

think of myself as your brother, I believe it is factually incorrect. For you and me to be brothers, we must either be genetically related, or one of us must be *legally* adopted into the family. It is my solemn duty to report that we are not brothers and can never be, since you are a human being and I am simply an advanced, mobile computer."

I tried to end that dumbness right there.

"You are my brother," I told Norman, "and I can prove it."

"Processing . . . Processing . . . I think that would be impossible," he said. "But if it is your desire to try to do so I will not interfere."

"Well, um, uh . . ." Uh-oh, I spoke before my thoughts were able to catch up to my voice box. How could I prove that Norman was my brother? Come on, brain, I encouraged. Thinking . . . Thinking . . . Got it!

"A few weeks before you showed up in your box I dropped my laptop, and it wouldn't work until Dad fixed it," I said. "I was upset that it was broken, but I wasn't sad about it, and I wasn't worried that the laptop might be in pain. When it was in Dad's lab for a few days I was mad that I couldn't use it, but I didn't miss it, or go into the lab every ten minutes to see how it was doing." I took in a deep breath and saw that Norman was watching me very carefully.

"But with you, when you accidentally threw yourself

into a wall and hurt yourself, and when you caught the worm, I was really worried about you, and afraid you might be in pain. And I missed you when you were getting repaired and reprogrammed, and I was sad that we couldn't hang out together. I didn't feel any of that junk for my broken laptop. Also, when it looked like you were falling for Annie Bananas, I told you to stay away from her, like a brother would do. I'd never do something like that for a computer, advanced or not. For all those reasons, that's how I know you are my brother."

It got quiet, except for a tiny clicking sound from Norman.

"Because you treat me like you would treat a brother, that is how you know we are brothers?" the robot asked. "Like how you would treat Lucien if he were here?"

"Yes, that's exactly it," I said, suddenly feeling oddly goopy about Lucien, and Norman.

"Processing . . . Processing . . . ," Norman said. "I think I understand. Being someone's brother is not just about shared genetics or similar blueprints for design, but it is about treating each other like brothers, and caring for each other like brothers. Correct?"

"Yes," I said as goopiness had more of its goopy way with me.

The robot crawled out of his box, climbed up on my bed, and kissed me on the cheek. "Good night, brother," he said.

"Good night, brother," I said, feeling I might do something majorly girlish like start to cry. I'm not *that* good of a brother.

Norman went and settled into his box. And I had another big thought.

"That's more proof that you are my brother!" I said triumphantly. "Computers do not kiss their brothers good night. But brothers do." For once I figured out something before Norman did. Yay!

"Oui!" said the robot. "Now the second part of my question. Why exactly am I here?"

Argh!!!

38.

The next morning Dad dropped me off at school before going to work; he had decided that Norman could use more time off for testing and adjustments. It felt kind of weird, being dropped off. I had always been a ride-the-bus kind of kid. But suddenly I was a dropped-off-by-a-parent kind of kid. It was going to take some time to get used to it, I figured.

Annie ran up to me while I was getting books out of my locker. "Hi, Matt! Where's Norman, and why weren't you guys on the bus?" she demanded.

So I told her with all the excitement you might get from a sleepy turtle that Norman wouldn't be returning to school until next week, and that he and I were going to be getting rides from now on.

"There's plenty of room for me in your car, Matt," she hinted, smiling and batting her eyelashes at me. "Talk to your dad! I could sit between you and Norman. Wouldn't that be great?"

Sure. In the same way screaming nightmares are great.

Annie wiggled her nose. "By the way, I figured out what your big secret is," she announced.

But I didn't want to know what Annie knew, so I closed my locker, told her I was late for class, and took off down the hallway. Of course she followed me.

"I looked up the name of the worm Norman said he caught, the Doomsday Sandwich worm, on the Internet," she said. "It's a computer worm. Norman is a *computer.* Make that a computerized robot! Ha! I figured it out!"

Dog poop served with a side of french fries and coleslaw!

But I put on a poker face. "You're insane," I told her, scrambling to think of something smart to say. "Um . . . Robotics isn't that advanced yet. The only robots we have are those machines that can vacuum rugs or mow lawns. It will probably be a hundred years before we have robots that look and act like people." Not too bad, for eight thirty in the morning.

"Liar!" Annie said, narrowing her eyes. "Norman being a robot makes perfect sense. Like how he can do gymnastic things that no other kid can do, how he's smarter than the rest of us, and how he knows every language ever invented. Robot! And I'm going to tell everyone." Then she paused, a better idea clearly coming to her. "Unless you do something for *me.*"

Oh no. This was going to be bad. What if she wanted me to kiss her, or something just as out-of-this-world gross, like hold her hand? No way! But I quickly realized that if I just ignored Annie, my usual strategy, she really would tell everyone that Norman was a bot. Don't believe it? Just look at her relentless pursuit of me! She's ruthless!

"What do you want to stay quiet?" I asked as we turned down a hallway.

"So Norman *is* a robot. Nailed it!" she cried.

I thought fast. "I'm not saying he's a robot, but it would be bad for Norman if people started thinking he was one. What do you want to keep your mouth shut? Spill it, Bananas."

"Easy, Matt," she said, with what I can only describe as a sinister smile. "I want us to go out. You know, dating. Boyfriend and girlfriend."

"I'm not allowed to date until I'm eighteen," I told her, trying to look bummed out. Actually, I wasn't sure that was true. I hadn't talked about that subject with Mom or Dad, but eighteen sounded right to me. "Ask for something else."

"Darn it!" she said, frowning and doing some thinking. It's not the easiest thing, watching Annie Bananas think. I always feel bad for her puny brain.

The class bell rang and saved me. I slipped inside my homeroom, and Annie hurried to hers. *Phew!*

*   *   *

Jeter and I were at our lunch table, talking about the mystery of boogers—how exactly they're formed, and why the different colors, and their amazing finger-clinging abilities—when Annie stopped by and sat next to me.

"Girl alert!" Jeter said, a million years too late.

Might as well get this over with, I thought. "What do you want?" I asked Annie.

She giggled. "I want you to stand on your table and shout to the entire lunchroom, 'I'm crazy in love with beautiful Annie Bonano.'"

No way! Jeter laughed so hard and quick he was suddenly snotty.

"How about you just stab me in the arm with a fork?" I said. There are times when a flesh wound is the lesser of two evils.

"Nope," she said. "Say you're in love with me and I'll keep the secret. Come on! I'm waiting."

Oh boy, oh boy, oh boy.

Hoping this wasn't going to be as horrible as I knew it would be, I set my fork down, climbed onto the table, and stood up. I was hoping no one would notice me—there was a lot of jabbering going on just ten seconds earlier—but wouldn't you know it, the lunchroom had gone quiet while hundreds of eyes gazed at me. *Gulp.*

"Uh, hey," I said, stalling to give time for Jeter, or a

sudden earthquake, or a rip in the time-space contin-uum if this was a cheesy episode of *Star Trek*, to stop me.

No such luck.

"So guess what, everybody," I said in a normal voice.

"Louder!" Annie hissed, so I cranked up the volume.

"I'm crazy in love with beautiful Annie Bonano!" I nearly shouted, disbelieving that those words had actu-ally come out of my mouth. I had just confessed love to a she-devil. Stupid mouth!

"Hurray!" Annie said, clapping like a goof.

When I returned to my seat, she kissed me on my

cheek. More bleck! I wiped at my face and gave her my fiercest look. "We've got a deal now," I reminded her. She smiled happily, jumped up, and scooted back to her table. The other kids went back to jabbering and eating. I guess they were expecting a bigger announcement from me, like the United Nations had just declared the rest of the day a school holiday. Everyone go home!

"That was totally weird, what you just did," Jeter said, shaking his bangs away from his face. "I didn't know you liked Annie. You dog! Why didn't you tell me? I'm your best friend!"

Did I mention that Jeter is not the brightest kid on earth? Or even in the top billion?

"It was a sudden crush," I said. "It's already worn off."

Before I could get to math class, Principal Jackson pulled me into his office. I guessed that standing on the lunch table was off-limits, and I wondered who ratted me out. Maybe that one lunch lady who got all huffy when I asked her to check if there was more chocolate pudding in back, when there was none left up front. She didn't check. But hey, I just knew there were big barrels of pudding somewhere in back.

As soon as we were seated, Principal J. started talking about "the roller coaster ride" that is adolescence, and how "jumpy hormones" had caused many young men to "engage in highly erratic behavior," and how it was important that we "restrain our passions" while on school grounds, and for that matter while off school grounds.

I just sort of nodded to speed things along, thinking I truly understood the meaning of the word "mortified."

And then Principal Jackson said that standing on lunch tables was a "hygiene and safety issue," so if it happened again he would have no choice but to call my parents and give me a detention. Since I'm hoping to be one of those kids who skates through middle school and high school detention free, I promised that I would never for the rest of my life stand on a table and say I love a girl. I even crossed my heart.

"Very good." He nodded and leaned a little closer. I sensed a Norman question coming on. "So how is Norman doing?" he asked. Yup, I was right. "For some reason this place just doesn't seem as lively when he's not here. Norman is an exceptional child."

Yes, he truly is. So exceptional he comes with a warranty!

"He'll be back next week," I assured him. "He just needs a few more software updates." Argh! What was wrong with my mouth?

But Principal J. just laughed and waved an arm at me. "You kids and your computer lingo. When I was your age, personal computers were the size of this office and were programmed by cards with holes punched in them. Ah, those were the days." He leaned back and seemed to be having a sentimental moment. I took that as my cue to get out of there and head to class.

On the way to math I kept my eyes open for fake janitors, wonky security guards, holographic hall monitors, and so on. Nothing. Was it possible that the spies had given up their mission, whatever that mission was? Didn't know, but I sure as heck hoped so.

As it turned out . . . Well, please stay tuned—it's almost time for the good stuff. (Yeah, I know, I hate waiting for the good stuff too, but my mom says it's important when telling stories to relate the events in the proper order so people don't get confused. So, um . . . blame her!)

39.

Halloween is probably my favorite holiday. I mean, you get to dress up like a superhero or a movie character or a werewolf and run around at night with your friends, and people literally throw candy at you for two whole hours. Perfect! Too bad it only comes once a year.

This was Norman's first Halloween—obviously! While Norman had no use for candy, Dad thought it would be a good idea if Jeter and I took him along with us for trick or treat so he could feel like one of the kids. Norman wasn't all the way back; Dad said he might never be exactly like we remember him, but he did seem much less completely robot-y.

Still, before Norman would agree to go with us, he wanted to discuss the "logic" of Halloween. "*Pardonne-moi*, Matt," he said. "While I understand why children would find amusement in dressing up in costumes and collecting sugary items from their neighbors, I do not understand the motivation of the adults handing out snacks without requesting compensation. Even a small fee to cover their expenses would be reasonable."

"Because it's a tradition?" I said, but Norman wasn't buying it.

"Because it's fun giving kids free candy?" I tried, but Norman just shook his head. So I threw in the towel.

"Maybe you could come along and help us figure out what their motivation is," I said.

"If it is possible that my research may lead to a greater understanding of this strange social phenomenon, then I am happy to participate," he said.

Yeah, my brother was still a little weird.

I was an ogre this year. Sort of like Shrek, except meaner-looking and without the weird horns.

My costume was easy to put together. All I needed was an eye patch and a furry vest, which I found at a thrift shop. And then I painted green makeup on my face and arms. Naturally, Mom took several pictures of me.

"Say cheese," Mom said, from behind a camera. But I said "owls" instead of "cheese." It seemed more of an ogrelike thing to say. A true ogre probably wouldn't eat cheese. But he might eat owls.

Oh. Jeter was dressed as a pirate. Just like last year, and the year before, and the year before that one . . .

Norman, even though I was willing to lend him my Iron Man mask from last year, decided he wanted to dress up like Napoleon Bonaparte, "a most influential person in the history of my beloved France." His beloved France? He was just built there! Norman lives in the good old USA.

You can't buy a Napoleon costume at Target or Macy's, so Dad had to drive to a costume rental shop in Brooklyn to find the right outfit for Norman. I wasn't sure that was fair. Mom or Dad never rented a costume for me to wear. Not that I ever asked them to.

Norman did look pretty good in his Napoleon Bonaparte costume, especially with the funny hat and fake sword. Okay, I might have been a tiny bit jealous that I didn't think of the Napoleon costume first. I was just a dumb ogre, probably one of a thousand ogres roaming the streets and apartment buildings of New York City.

After posing for yet another picture, Jeter, Norman, and I were about to go collect a month's worth of candy when there was a loud pounding at the door. Crud! I sighed extra miserably, then opened the door and saw Annie Bananas in a pink fairy costume with all sorts of glitter. She was also holding a silver wand. She's such a . . . girl!

"You weren't seriously thinking of going trick-or-treating without me, were you, Matt?" she said, smiling and showing off her teeth like they were prize emeralds. She then gazed at Norman like she was inspecting him for exposed wires or a Frankenstein-like neck bolt. I hated that she knew that Norman is a bot. It was like she held all the cards.

I peered at Dad. His little nod told me there was no point in fighting it, that Annie could come along with us. So I didn't fight it. I figured that I should save all my strength for mass candy eating, anyway.

In Manhattan, most kids trick-or-treat in their own buildings. Since we have twelve floors, and Mom and Dad don't like doing all that walking and stair climbing, the rule is that I can choose odd-numbered floors or even-numbered floors to go begging. I went with odd-numbered floors. It was just feeling like an odd kind of year.

So we were officially trick-or-treating, or as Jeter the pirate calls it, trick-*rrr*-treating—he says that dumb joke every year—passing a few kids dressed as witches and ghosts on the first floor. Mom and Dad were strolling behind us. They seemed to be in a lovey-dovey mood, holding hands and making eyes at each other. That was one of those things that was more cool than gross, but it was still partway gross.

The first apartment we stopped at belonged to Mr. Dewey. He's the kind of neighbor you see all the time but hardly ever talk to. I've lived in this building my whole life and have maybe said ten words to the guy.

Annie knocked, and we waited. As soon as Mr. Dewey opened his door, Norman said, "*Bonjour*, kind neighbor. My brother and his friends and I are here so we can better understand the intricacies of the annual ritual known as Halloween, more specifically the experience of what is commonly referred to as 'trick-or-treating.' Would you be so kind as to further our research by way of offering nonperishable snack items without any charge to us?"

Mr. Dewey looked dumbly at Annie, Jeter, and me. "Trick or treat," we said. Clearly relieved, Mr. Dewey reached for a bowl of mini candy bars and shoved it out the door. The four of us snagged candy. While the unwritten rule is one candy bar per kid, if you move your hand really fast while other kids' hands are in the bowl, you can sometimes get away with snagging two or even three bars. So yeah, I grabbed two Milky Ways and wasn't busted. Victory is mine!

Mr. Dewey closed the door on us.

"That was invigorating, being offered a high-calorie treat without the need for compensating the giver of said treat," Norman said as we shuffled to the next apartment. "Will we be returning later so I may ask the gentleman several research questions about his Halloween practices and perceptions?"

"Uh, sure," I said, "or maybe next week would be better. You know, so there's time to take notes." That seemed to satisfy Norman.

The next apartment we stopped at belonged to a raisiny woman named Old Lady Ireland. She probably has a first name like Maude or Millie, but I don't know what it is. Old Lady Ireland is the opposite of Mr. Dewey, one of those neighbors who is always talking to you, even if you are hurrying to the bus stop or are otherwise trying to get away from her as quickly as possible.

She's also a cheapo. For the treat she gave each of us one tiny pack of SweeTarts, with maybe two candies inside. It almost wasn't worth the trouble.

Then Old Lady Ireland asked Norman who he was dressed as. So Norman went into this rant about the great Napoleon Bonaparte and the French Revolution, which probably would have been interesting if there wasn't all that candy waiting to be collected and only so much time to collect it. I had to pull Norman away from the door. While I was doing that, the old woman thanked the robot for the "fascinating history lesson" and invited him to come back anytime to continue the discussion. I think she must be lonely.

"*Oui, madame,* I would be most excited to return in the very near future," Norman said while I was tugging him down the hall. "*Vive la France!*"

Now it was just getting weird.

By the time we reached the fifth floor, the haul had already been pretty good. Though on the third floor a man was handing out healthy candy bars called Soy

Nut Blast! *Bleck.* I decided to hide that one in case there was some sort of horrible catastrophe affecting the food supply, and I had to eat something almost edible to survive.

Anyway, we were approaching apartment 5A when . . . *Wonk! Wonk! Wonk!*

Crud! The fire alarm had been set off. Even though there was probably no actual fire—I didn't smell any smoke—the rule was we had to clear the building until the fire department gave the okay to return. Sometimes that took an hour, or longer. By then trick or treat would be over.

"Let's go, kids," Dad said, as he and Mom corralled us toward the stairs.

"Of all the rotten luck," I grumbled as we descended the stairs along with a bunch of other kids and parents. I was expecting Mom or Dad to remind me of all the starving kids in the world who couldn't even dream of something like trick or treat, but that time I caught a break.

Wonk! Wonk! Wonk!

Norman elbowed me in the side. "Excuse me, Matt," he said urgently. "That is not an air raid alert, is it?"

"Nah, it's just a fire alarm," I told him. "Some guy probably burned his toast and set off a smoke alarm. It's nothing to worry about."

A few seconds passed, then Norman smiled. "Toasted toast?" he said, letting out a *th-th-th-th-th* snicker.

Whoa. Did the robot attempt a joke? It was almost funny!

Soon my family and friends and I were outside on the sidewalk, along with dozens of other building residents, waiting for the fire department to show up. It was a weird mix of the bummed and the bored, many of them in costumes. Sometimes strangers tramping by would stop for a minute or two, looking up at the building like they were expecting to see something suitable for a disaster movie. Others just scooted along, ignoring the crowd. And then there was Leon, the super, periodically flapping his arms around like a choral director and saying, "Everyone please stay calm." But I didn't think that anyone was about to freak. Annie Bananas even looked kind of smiley-happy, like the fire alarm going off was the perfect development. I just don't understand that girl.

At least it wasn't raining, or snowing. That would have smelled.

Finally I saw a fire truck heading our way, though it was still a few blocks down the street. "Hey, Norman," I said, "do you—" Norman? Where the heck was Norman?

I looked around in a panic and spotted my brother walking away with two men wearing clown masks. Ack! I was pretty sure it was those two guys, the spies. "Norman, get back here!" I shouted. Then to my dad I said more quietly, "Dad! It's them! Those guys!"

As I dashed to Norman, the one man grabbed at my brother, but he broke away from him and the men took off running, through the crowd and down the street. Dad caught up to us.

"It was them! Those spy guys!" I cried. "They almost had Norman!" It felt like I had enough energy to fly to the moon. You know, with my arms.

Dad peered down the street, but the men were gone. Anger took over his face. He grabbed the robot firmly by his shoulders. "Norman!" he scolded. "I told you to never talk to strangers!"

"But the men said that they had an urgent matter they wished to discuss with me," Norman said, blinking a few times. "I only wanted to be helpful."

"I don't care if someone tells you that the fate of the world is in your hands," Dad hissed. "You do NOT talk to strangers EVER! Got it?"

I wasn't sure if Norman had figured out the crying thing yet, but it sure looked like he was about to give it another try. "*Oui*, Papa," he said. "My apologies."

One good thing about my dad and anger, they never stay together very long. Dad exhaled and melted a little, seeming more like his normal self. "At least it turned out okay, this time," he said. He glanced back down the street. "But that was a little too close." And I wondered if he suspected what I suspected, that those men were the ones who'd set off the fire alarm.

Lumbering back to Mom, Annie, and Jeter, Dad gave me a look that said we were maybe a minute from losing Norman, something I already knew but didn't want to think about. If that happened, if we lost Norman . . . I'd cry for a freakin' year.

Even though we were cleared to go back inside with nearly fifteen minutes left for trick-or-treating, Dad decided that Halloween was over for us. "We'll make up for it next year, kids," he said, throwing on a smile that could barely keep itself upright. He then went back to fending off questions from Mom about what had happened with Norman and the two men in clown masks. He promised to tell her everything once we were safely inside our apartment. Mom kept pushing. Dad kept waffling.

"Is something going on I don't know about?" Jeter whispered to me as we all headed inside the building.

"Lots of things," I said. It was tough keeping secrets from my best friend. So if Jeter asked more questions, I decided that I was going to spill the beans about Norman, the spies, everything. Besides, I didn't expect Annie to keep a secret this big much longer. When we were trick-or-treating on the third floor, she'd nudged me in the side and quietly asked if Norman would need to be recharged soon. It was just a matter of time before the secret was out.

But instead of pressing me for answers, Jeter checked his bag of candy, already distracted. His tiny attention span really rots when we are playing video or board games, but at times like this it sure came in handy. "Aye, quite a bounty this year," he said with a pirate snarl. "Warms the cockles of me seafaring pirate heart."

That's my Jeter!

40.

While my mom and dad continued "conferencing" in the kitchen, Annie, Norman, Jeter, and I were in my room, counting our candy. It was strange having Annie in my room. I was thinking about getting the place fumigated.

"Hey, why is there only one bed?" Annie asked, looking around. "Doesn't Norman sleep in here too?"

Before I could say anything, Norman pointed to his crate. "I have found that packaging materials and a wooden chamber provide a superior sleep-mode experience than can be found by utilizing a bed or a couch, or even a toy box."

"Should have figured," Annie said, rolling her eyes.

As it turned out, Norman had a LOT more candy than the rest of us. People at nearly every apartment we'd stopped at clearly preferred his costume. That sucked. I was out-trick-or-treated by a rookie.

Anyway, back to the feast. Just as I was wondering if I might be able to talk Norman out of some of his candy, he pushed his treats toward Annie, Jeter, and me.

"Help yourself," he said. "I have no interest in this candy now that my field research is completed for the evening."

"*Rrrr*, that's mighty fine of you, lad," Jeter said as we divided Norman's candy. "A fine pirate ye are. May ye never walk the plank!"

Sometimes the pirate thing was a little annoying.

And then the big debate: Should I start with a mini Three Musketeers, or eat the candy corn first? Or maybe some peanut M&M's to begin the festivities . . .

The conferencing in the kitchen turned into a shouting match. Ugh. There is almost nothing worse than having your parents fight when your friends are over. Do they have *any* clue how embarrassing it is?

I didn't hear what my dad said, but my mom yelled something about how Dad "brought this danger to our doorstep," and now it was time to "step up and do the right thing for this family."

The candy corn (made my decision) went sour in my mouth. Could my parents be thinking of shipping Norman back to France? That would be terrible! Now I couldn't even swallow. But if they wanted Norman gone, he was gone. Adults ruled the world, and this family.

I spat the orange and yellow mush into a Kleenex. Annie, seeing this, *eww*ed.

The fight kept going on, and we heard lots of it. Annie and Jeter looked like they felt bad for me. I felt bad for me. While I was trying to think of a way to save the day, Norman beat me to it by singing, totally out of the blue, that one French song.

"*Alouette, gentille Alouette, Alouette, je te plumerai.*"

To my surprise, Jeter and Annie joined in. So I did too, all of us cranking it up so we drowned out my mom and dad. I think that's something every kid—even a robot kid—understands, that yelling parents *must* be drowned out no matter what, even if singing a silly French song about plucking a dead bird is your best option.

"*Je te plumerai la tête, Je te plumerai la tête, Et la tête, et la tête . . . Alouette, gentille Alouette, Alouette, je te plumerai . . .*"

41.

Jeter was picked up by his dad, and I was finally able to talk Annie into going home to her own apartment. And then it was time for a family meeting at the dining table. But it wasn't a complete family meeting: Norman was in the lab, hooked up to a computer and having his files checked for viruses, worms, and spyware.

Like most family meetings, Mom was in charge. Dad was peering down at his shoes like they were his only friends. I could tell before the first word was said that this meeting was not going to be fun. Not that they ever were . . .

"Your father finally told me everything that has been going on with Norman and Jean-Pierre Junior," Mom said to me, "and the people who might be trying to harm them, or otherwise have a suspicious interest in the robots. So now we have to decide what to do about Norman."

What was there to decide? "We protect Norman," I said. "Keep him safe."

"Yes, but it's not that simple," Mom said. "Norman living here is a threat to all of us. Who knows what these people are capable of, beyond designing computer worms and spying. They even tried to snatch up Norman! As far as I'm concerned, any threat to this family must be dealt with aggressively. Waiting to see what these people might do next would be the worst thing to do."

Dad spoke up. "Tomorrow I'm going to file a report with the police about these two men. If the cops can find them, I'm pretty sure they have enough to make an arrest."

"But what if the police don't find them?" Mom said. "If these men took the trouble to wear disguises, infiltrate Matt's school, and everything else they've done . . . Clearly they are not amateurs, nor afraid to take chances to accomplish their goals."

"But involving the cops *could* put an end to it," Dad said.

"But it might not, which is my point," Mom said. "Whether these people want to destroy the robots or steal the technology for their own purposes, they probably won't stop until someone stops them, or they get what they are after. The thing is, the rest of us could be harmed by whatever they are planning. We need to do whatever we have to do to keep that from happening."

I knew it. My mom was thinking about getting rid of Norman. I looked wildly toward Dad.

He glanced at me, then quickly shifted his eyes. "Your mother and I have been discussing the possibility of sending Norman away."

"Sending him where?" I asked, knowing full well they were not talking about a prep school or a military academy.

"Back to France, for . . . proper disassembly," my father told me. "The same thing will happen with Jean-Pierre Junior if your uncle agrees. We *cannot* let this technology fall into the wrong hands."

"No way," I nearly shouted. You don't give a kid a brother, then send him back to France for disassembly. "Norman is part of our family," I went on. "We can't just send him away."

To my total shock, Mom said, "Yes, he is part of this family." But then she said, "But if we had a dog that was part of this family and he suddenly turned vicious, was threatening to harm any one of us, I would get rid of him that day. Sometimes we have to look at the bigger picture. No one was spying on us or hacking our computers until Norman showed up, Matt."

But . . . but . . . I was getting madder by the minute. "Norman is a person, not a dog!"

"Honey, not really," Mom said. "Norman is like a person, and we've all grown fond of him, but he is, essentially, an extraordinary machine. And a machine, no matter how clever, isn't the same thing as a person."

A quiet, heavy moment. That was how these family meetings went, Mom and Dad giving me "space" to vent words and feelings, even if those words and feelings didn't end up changing anything.

I decided to throw a grenade. "If someone was trying to harm me, would you send me to France for disassembly?" I asked.

"No, of course not," Mom said. "But—"

"Norman is my brother," I quickly said, before Mom could load more ammo. "So I think we need to stick together as a family, no matter what happens." It's weird when you're talking with your parents and you, the kid, are the only one making sense.

Mom peered at Dad, who gave a shrug so tiny it was more like a twitch.

Mom sighed.

Dad rubbed his face.

"Guys, it's been a long day and it's getting late," Mom said. "How about we see what happens with the police tomorrow morning, and then decide what to do?"

Dad nodded. I nodded. But none of us seemed any less upset. Despite all my moaning, all I probably did was buy Norman one more day in New York. And that just stank.

42.

Norman was asleep in his box. I was trying to sleep, but it wasn't working. I was too busy worrying about Norman, and what would happen to him if he was shipped back to France, and also what might happen if he stayed and somehow the spies got him.

"Hey, Norman, please wake up," I said. Norman's eyes blinked open. Thank goodness he has voice activation. Having to press a button to wake him up would have been freaky.

"Yes, Matthew?" he said. "Is there something you wish to discuss?"

"Um, sort of," I said, trying to find some courage. "It's just that I want to say that I really like having you around, okay?"

The only thing worse than feeling mushed-out is having to talk about your mushed-outedness with some-one. But I thought Norman should know this, just in case he was about to be sent to France and taken apart.

"*Merci*, Matt," Norman said. "I believe that I now have

a greater understanding of brotherly love, the process where siblings develop fondness and protective feelings toward each other. It means that you would take a bullet for me, as they say in the movies, yes?"

A bullet? Yikes! "Sure, why not," I said, hoping that a taking-a-bullet-for-Norman opportunity never showed up. Maybe a BB wouldn't be so bad, but a bullet?

"And I would take a disabling power surge for you, brother," Norman said.

I was glad that was settled. "Why thank you, Norman," I said. "G'night."

"Good night, Matt," he said.

"Wait! I keep meaning to ask: Do you dream? Or see anything when you close your eyes at night?"

"*Oui.* I see strings of numbers and symbols when in sleep mode." Just as I was thinking, *Boring!* the robot added, "And they are so very beautiful."

Whatever works for you, Norman.

My brother closed his eyes and powered down. I tried to do the same.

45.

Things got weirdly quiet, just when I was expecting a big, noisy storm.

My dad filed a police report, but even though they stationed an extra cop on our block—apparently the NYPD takes potential child-nappings very seriously— the police were not able to find the spies. But hey, this is a city of eight million people. One of the cops told Dad that if they did find the men, he wasn't sure they had enough to file charges. "If we locked up every- one who likes to dress in bizarre outfits and exhibit strange behavior," the cop said, "half of New York would be in jail."

Norman was still living with us and was back in school. I had a good talk with him, and he wasn't much of a show-off anymore. Basically, I explained that it was fine to do well in his classes, but if he came across as supersmart and athletic, that made the rest of us look a little dumb and cloddy. "So can you turn it down a notch or two when we are at school, buddy?" I pleaded.

"*Oui,* I will turn it down two notches," he said. "Try to be more of an average Joseph."

So in gym, Norman struggled to do ten push-ups, like the rest of us skinny kids.

In math, when Mr. Porter asked Norman to do an equation, he pulled out a calculator and used it, even though I was sure he knew the answer.

In computer studies, Norman passed on a chance to repair a busted computer, saying he was not a certified technician.

Which meant that Norman was being treated like any other not-so-athletic, not-so-brainy kid by the other kids and the teachers and by Principal Jackson. I liked that much better. To be honest, it was a big pain having a brother who was loads smarter and more popular than I was. But I would have dealt with it, as long as Norman got to stay with us.

Some news. Feeling a little better about how things were going, and egged on by Norman—"You have excellent leadership skills," he weirdly insisted—I decided to take a big step and run for student council as the sixth-grade representative. I saw a flycr announcing an upcoming election to replace Jill Peppercorn, the former sixth-grade rep—Jill and her family had moved to Albany for unknown reasons—and thought why not give it a shot? Plus, usually only nerds and total rejects run for things like student council, and stacked up against nerds and total rejects, I look pretty good. And no one else had signed up for the election yet, which like doubled my odds of success.

My platform? If elected I would demand that the soda machine be returned to the lunchroom. It was replaced last month by a juice machine. I know juice is healthier than soda, but I think kids twelve and older should be allowed to make their own beverage choices. We aren't robots; we like to make up our own minds about stuff. I mean *most of us* are not robots.

I've also been thinking of starting an annual Stinky Sneaker Day, where the school would have a contest for the smelliest sneaker, judged by a panel of kids and teachers with big noses. The winner would get a day off from school and a trophy in the shape of a sneaker.

But a Stinky Sneaker Day would probably be squashed by Principal Jackson before it could get started. Adults excel at ruining all the fun.

So life had pretty much gotten back to semi-normal, which was about the most I could hope for. But then one morning, a Friday . . . Cue the oogles!

Here we go. The good stuff.

After finishing breakfast and getting dressed for school, Norman and I headed to the lab to hang out with Dad. When you're a kid with busy parents, you have to grab quality family time whenever you can.

Inside the lab I saw that my dad was grading student papers. Norman, meanwhile, zipped over to the computer and started a video chat with Jean-Pierre Jr.

"Good morning, Dad," I said, on the heels of a giant yawn.

"Morning?" he asked, spaced-out. "That's right, it's morning. What a wonderful time of day."

Um, okay.

I slipped past my dad and moved closer to Norman— he was yakking with Jean-Pierre Jr. about a recent language module upgrade. On the screen behind Jean-Pierre Jr., I saw my uncle reading a computer manual in the same way my mom read mystery novels, like he was itching to flip the page and find out what happened next.

Naturally, Norman and Jean-Pierre Jr. were talking in French. I was at least 78 percent lost.

It was actually kind of boring, and I was trying to think of something else I could do. But then it turned unboring very quickly.

Gazing at the monitor, I saw two men in black sweat-shirts, jeans, and sunglasses busting into my uncle's computer room.

"Uh! Uh! Dad! Look!" I yelled. He dropped his pen and moved closer to the computer. We stared in shock as one of the men put a hand over my uncle's mouth and started dragging him away from the computer. And the second man was coming toward us with his hand. The screen went black. He covered the camera!

"Jean-Pierre Junior! Jean-Pierre Junior!" Norman cried frantically. "*Parle-moi, cousin!* Speak to me!"

But there was only an error message on the screen, saying that the connection had been lost.

"Dad! Do something!" I said, fear fizzing inside me.

But he was already sitting down at the computer next to Norman, who looked stunned, like he couldn't process what he'd just seen. Dad quickly typed something on the keyboard, but got a different error message saying that the "target address" was offline and unavailable.

Fortunately, my dad knows a way around almost all error messages. He madly typed some more, and soon he was reconnected to Uncle Jean-Pierre's computer camera. But it showed only an empty room.

"*Mon dieu,*" Norman said. "What happened to my uncle and my cousin? Who are those awful men?"

Dad jumped up. "Okay, we're not going to panic, but we have to get out of here immediately." He took both of our arms and steered us toward the door. "Whoever those people are, their associates may now be coming for us. Let's get your mother and go."

My heart was beating so loud I could hear it. I took Norman's hand. But then my dad slowed down at the doorway and whipped out his cell phone.

"Hello?" he said, after dialing. "I need to be immediately connected to Interpol. It's an emergency. . . . You must—Hello? Hello?" (Interpol, in case you don't know, is the International Police Agency.) He held the phone away from his face, then showed the screen to Norman and me. A string of frowning faces rolled across it. "Someone is blocking the signal," he said, staring at the screen with a stunned expression. "That's just . . . advanced. Even I don't know how to do that."

He asked to borrow my phone, but it was the same story, frowning faces but no signal. "My God. Just what are these people capable of?" he asked. I could hear the fear in his voice.

At our apartment door, Dad was about to push it open just as Mom was pulling it open. "There you guys are," she said, smiling, but then the lightness faded from her face. "What's going on? You guys look like you just saw a ghost."

"We have to leave, right now!" Dad told Mom, taking her arm. "Something terrible has happened to Jean-Pierre and Jean-Pierre Junior! And we may be in immediate danger too. They're jamming our cell phones!"

Mom's mouth fell open. "What happened?" she asked. "And who exactly are 'they'?"

"We think they were kidnapped," I told her. "We saw it happen on the cam. Norman and Jean-Pierre Junior were just—"

"Honey, we have to go. Now!" Dad interrupted. "It's possible their associates—those two men we talked about, I'm betting—may be coming for us."

"Kidnapped? Jammed cell phones?" My mother stared frantically at my father.

"We have to go!" Dad said. He patted at his back pocket to make sure he had his wallet, then pulled at Mom's arm, as if trying to jump-start her. "This could be a matter of life and death."

Ack!

Mom nodded and we were on our way. At the elevator, Dad urgently pushed the down button. The doors opened a few seconds later. Empty. We hurried inside, where my dad pushed the button for the first floor like eleven times. The doors seemed to take forever to close.

"This is crazy," Mom said. "I just wanted to see what you guys were up to. And now . . ." She looked like she was about to lose it. Dad squeezed her hand.

"*Excusez-moi,*" Norman said. "But are these recent developments my fault?"

Mom, Dad, and I didn't answer. How do you tell a kid that his existence could be endangering his family? I sure couldn't think of any good way.

The elevator stopped on the second floor, and we all tensed up. When the doors opened, it was just a young guy wearing bicycle shorts and a T-shirt, sucking on a Vitaminwater. Dad gave the man the kind of look that captured my thoughts perfectly: *Take the stairs next time, jogger dude!*

On the first floor we hurried out of the elevator and then out the front door, where we all came to a dead stop. What was the plan? I wondered. Hop on a bus? Run to the subway? Flag down a taxi?

"To the Blue Bomber!" Dad said, lifting his index finger into the air. Mom rolled her eyes, but soon we were dashing to the parking garage behind our building, Norman grabbing my hand to help speed me along. Thanks, bro. My body just wasn't used to so much excitement that early in the day.

Inside the garage we scurried to the elevator and rode it to the top. I think the rent is cheaper up there. All the nicer cars are on the lower levels.

On the top deck we hurried to the Bomber, also known as the little blue 1992 Renault Clio that, many years ago, Dad gave Mom and some other students a lift to the Paris art museum in. When Mom and Dad moved to New York, Dad had it shipped here from France for "sentimental reasons." It used to be a broken-down beater, but then Dad had it restored so we'd have a working car for whenever we needed one.

"I guess the Clio will have to do," Mom said, sighing. She never liked riding in the Renault. About as safe as a refrigerator with wheels, she once said.

We scooted to the car, then Dad handed the keys to Mom. "Maybe you should drive," he told her. "I'm pretty much in full-throttle freak-out mode."

"And I'm the calm one?" Mom said, but she took the keys.

Climbing inside the Renault, I was thinking two things. First, I wished there had been time to hit the bathroom before we ran for our lives. Second, if anyone chased us, they would probably catch us. Mom was no NASCAR driver, the car was old and slow, and this was New York City. Even the highways get clogged up here.

44.

Soon we were heading south through Manhattan, passing Zabar's deli. If you're ever in New York City, make sure you try one of their poppy-seed bagels. They are out of this world! But, um, I think I've gotten off track. Where was . . . Oh. Norman and I were squeezed together in back, watching for spies.

I can't speak for Norman or my parents, but I remember thinking, *This is totally nuts.* Just twenty minutes earlier I was a normal kid living a pretty normal life, even if I did have a robotic brother. And I never once thought of myself as a run-for-his-life-with-his-family kind of kid. But there I was, running for my life with my family.

"Where should we go?" Mom asked, checking the mirrors. So often I worried that she'd forget to look straight ahead.

"I'm not sure yet," Dad said. "Just keep driving. We'll figure it out as we go." He started filling Mom in on what we'd seen happen to Jean-Pierre Sr. and Jr. on the computer.

This was scary. Not exciting scary or cool scary or even interesting scary. Just scary scary, the worst kind of scary.

I looked to Norman for some robot-style comfort, but suddenly he tensed up and his face went blank, like all his Norman-ness was gone. What the heck? Before I could tell Dad, Norman started talking in a weird, deep, adult voice. "If you know what's good for you, Rambeau family," he said, "pull to the side of the road and hand over the robot. Pull over right now!"

Somehow, life just got even scarier.

"Matthew . . . who is that?" Mom said in a panicky voice. "What's the matter with Norman?"

"Let me think, okay?" Dad said. "They—they must be speaking through one of Norman's communication portals. But which one?"

"Ah! They have to be right on us!" Mom said, looking all around.

"Or they could be tracking us from blocks or even a mile or more away," Dad said. "Everyone keep your eyes out for—"

"A silver Audi," I said, finishing his sentence and checking every car I could see, northbound and southbound, parked and moving. Nothing suspicious yet.

Dad turned toward the robot. "Norman, disable your GPS tracking device, as well as your Bluetooth and LAN network capabilities," he ordered.

But it didn't do any good.

"Pull over immediately!" the voice speaking through Norman said. "Hand over the robot and no one will be harmed. Now!"

Yikes!

"Norman, this is a voice command override," my dad tried. "Immediately disable all communication portals and network capabilities."

No dice. The voice just repeated itself, saying we needed to stop the car and hand over the robot. Shoot! I knew that I had to try to help Norman somehow.

An idea . . .

I faced my brother, grabbed his arms, and gave him a good shake. "Norman, this is your brother, Matt," I said, in my most super-serious voice. "You *must* listen to Papa and disable your communication portals and network . . . thingies." I threw in a desperate, "Please, brother?"

A few seconds passed, then Norman blinked several times and said in his normal voice, "Communication portals and network 'thingies' disabled." He smiled but showed a puzzled look. *"Pardonne-moi,"* he said. "Did a glitch just occur? I am missing exactly one minute and forty-nine seconds of data from my short-term memory storage."

"I'll have to tell you later," Dad said to the robot. "We have more pressing matters." He looked to both sides, then behind us. "The spies must be getting closer."

More yikes!

45.

Columbus Circle was totally jammed with cars, buses, and taxis. That made me panic until I realized that if we were going slow, then the men chasing us were probably going just as slow.

Dad tried his cell phone again, then snapped it shut with frustration. "Everything is going to be fine," he said, but there wasn't more than an ounce of confidence in his voice.

And that was when a silver Audi wedged its way between a taxi and us. It was the two guys, the spies! Their right front window lowered, and I found myself looking at the cold eyes of one of the men. He quickly flashed a gun, then put it somewhere below the window. A gun! It was a gun! I was so frightened I even forgot to duck.

"It's them!" I shouted. "They're right next us! The one guy has a gun!"

The silver car then slipped behind our car. Dad peered out the rear window and told Mom to pick up speed.

"I'm doing the best I can," she said, focusing on the

traffic in front of us. "This is worse than rush hour. Why are there so many cars in this stupid city?" She slammed her hand against the steering wheel, then managed to pass a gray SUV. But the driver of the silver car did the same thing. They were still right on us.

I was trying to remember how to breathe.

Dad checked the side mirror, then turned toward Norman and me. "Matt," he said as serious as a brick. "I need you to leave Norman where he is and climb up front with us."

"Why?" I asked, sensing that I didn't want to know the answer.

"No arguments. Get up here," he demanded.

My right leg started to shake. I couldn't get it to stop. "I need to know why," I said to my dad, my voice going all crazy quivery.

Dad groaned, and told Norman to turn off his hearing. Norman blinked several times and said, "Hearing interface deactivated."

My dad rubbed his face and checked behind us again—the Audi was still there. "Norman has a voice-activated fail-safe mechanism," he told me, "to keep his technology from falling into the wrong hands. If certain code words and numbers are said, or typed in remotely, Norman will begin erasing files, then, essentially, implode, making it impossible for him to be rebuilt, or for his data to be recovered."

My brother was wired with explosives? Unreal! (But it was also kind of cool, in a weird way, having an explodable brother. Enough said!)

"You want to blow up Norman?" Mom asked, slowing down at an intersection. "In the car?!"

"Implode, not explode," Dad explained. "We should be perfectly safe, though Jean-Pierre and I never had a chance to test it. So the farther away we are from Norman, the better. Get up here, Matt."

"You can't blow up Norman!" I said as tears rushed to my eyes.

"I don't want to!" Dad said, his voice cracking. "But if I have to I will, to protect the technology, and you." He exhaled and patted at his face. "So please, please move Norman to the floor, as low as possible, then get up here just in case I need to say the code words."

He meant Lucien's birth date repeated twice. It somehow dawned on me that Lucien's birthday could be Norman's death day. How wrong was that?

I glanced at Norman, frozenly peering ahead, and knew what I had to do. I'm normally not the kind of kid who goes against what his parents tell him, but this was different. This was about Norman.

So I slipped my arm around my brother and pulled him closer. "You are *not* hurting Norman," I said. The clueless robot smiled at me. Aggh!

"Matthew!" my father exclaimed, gritting his teeth.

I didn't budge.

"Do what your father said, Matt!" Mom barked, checking the mirrors. "And where are the police? How can there not be one policeman on the street?" (That's one of the funky things about living in New York City. When you don't need a cop, it's like there's one on every corner. But when you do . . . Well, it's like they're all hanging out at the Donut Shack or something. Or, better, Zabar's deli.)

"Forget it," I said, feeling brave and weak at the same time, but knowing with absolute certainty that Norman would do the same for me.

Dad looked like he was about to implode himself, but then he gave a big sigh. "I guess I'd feel the same way if it was my brother who was at risk," he said, turning away from Norman and me. "Be safe, Jean-Pierre," he mumbled.

Phew! I sucked in air, then signaled Norman that it was okay to activate his hearing.

"Hearing interface engaged," the robot said, blinking. "I hope I did not miss anything vital."

Nope. Just me saving your life, brother.

Mom had to stop at a red light at West 48th Street. That was when the silver car bumped into the back of the Renault. Not a big, thuddy jerk, but more like a tap, like they were sending us a message.

When the light turned green, Mom got a fierce look on her face and floored it, but the Audi drove up beside us, then the man who'd showed the gun pointed out his window and motioned, like he wanted us to pull to the curb, in front of a Thai restaurant. They're everywhere!

"Do they think we're crazy?" Dad said. "Do NOT pull over."

"I know, I know!" Mom shouted. "Matthew, we have to lose them, and quick. We only have an eighth of a tank of gas left."

While we were all looking for a way out of this mess, Mom suddenly swerved into oncoming traffic, forcing other cars to get out of the way, and punched down on the gas. Ah! This was very dangerous! But it took the spies by surprise—they were several car lengths back now.

Mom then made a quick, illegal turn, causing some pedestrians to give us ugly looks, and a traffic cop to blow a whistle. It was smooth sailing for a block, then we ran into a huge traffic jam outside Times Square. We came to a dead stop. So had the cars in front of us, beside us, and behind us. We were even more trapped than we'd been a minute earlier.

Mom smacked at the steering wheel and said, "What was I thinking? I should have stayed on Ninth."

Dad, Norman, and I looked back. The silver car was three cars behind us.

"Just stay calm," my dad urged, but he looked more on the edge of a major freak-out than my mom. And the traffic hadn't moved.

I peered ahead and saw a crowd gathered, some of them jumping up and down or holding signs. I wasn't sure what was going on, so I craned my neck and looked up at a Jumbotron, and realized what was happening: It was a live broadcast of the *Wake Up, America* show, and Fig Ferrell was giving the weather forecast.

Thanks for clogging up traffic, Fig. Jerk!

But then an idea hit me.

A super-big idea!

An idea so huge you'd think it took four brains

working together to come up with it. Sure, it was going to be risky, but . . . I had to give it a shot. NOW.

I looked back to make sure the Audi wasn't any closer—it wasn't—then undid Norman's and my seat belts, grabbed his hand, told Mom and Dad, "We'll be at the studio. Find us!" and slipped out of the car with Norman. As we were hurrying away, I heard Dad shout, "Matthew! Get back here!"

Trust me, Dad. And Mom. And Norman. I took a quick look back. A taxi driver was yelling at the guys in the Audi as they tried to pull into his lane, even though there wasn't any room. Good! And then two cops were running up to our car just as my mom and dad were slipping out of it. Not sure what was going on, but I thought that we better not go back. The plan I came up with might be the best hope of saving Norman. I had to stick to it no matter what.

Norman and I weaved through the TV show crowd, but the closer we got to Fig Ferrell, the tougher it was to make progress. I guess these people weren't eager to give up a chance of getting their faces on TV. But we pressed forward with lots of *excuse me, excuse me, excuse me*'s, and were soon at the front, near the barricade they'd set up to protect Fig from crazed fans.

I think the show was on commercial. *Oh wait, check the Jumbotron, doofus.* The *Wake Up, America* show was actually doing a segment inside the studio where Nancy and a chef were making omelets, packing them with all sorts of veggies and cheeses and meats. Yum!

Outside, Fig, only ten feet from Norman and me, chatted with a blond-haired lady wearing a sweatshirt that said GO CORNHUSKERS! Um, okay. Anyway, it was time to activate my plan. *Be brave*, I told myself.

"Hey, Fig," I yelled out. "How would you like to meet my robotic brother?"

This got Fig's attention. He lumbered to us, glancing at Norman and me. "A robotic brother, huh?" he said, squeezing his face into a doubtful look. "So what is he going to do, break out in a robot dance?"

"Not exactly," I said, tugging Norman closer and lifting up a flap of his neck skin, revealing ports and his power button. A few people in the crowd oohed or said things like "That's weird," or even backed away from us a little.

Fig was not impressed. "While I'll admit that the computer gizmo stuff is peculiar," he said, "all I can say is good one, guys. Nice job of fakery. But sorry, I've seen it all. I'm not putting you on camera."

He started to leave. Time to crank it up. "Norman, go into hyper robot mode," I told my brother. "Right now. Show us your mad skills!"

"*Oui,*" Norman said, grinning. He then did a dozen

standing backflips while reciting lines from the Shake-speare play *Hamlet*, first in English . . .

> To be, or not to be: that is the question:
> Whether 'tis nobler in the mind to suffer
> The slings and arrows of outrageous fortune,
> Or to take arms against a sea of troubles,
> And by opposing end them?

And then he said it in French, which I won't even bother trying to repeat.

After that, he dropped to the ground and started doing rapid-fire push-ups with one pinkie while explaining the law of gravity and reciting a brief biography of the great Sir Isaac Newton.

Next, the robot folded himself into a ball and rolled toward a flagpole, which he climbed as fast as Spider-Man could—pretty much a blur—while multiplying *pi* times *pi* times *pi*. "*Pi* times *pi* equals 9.8696044, times *pi* equals 31.0062766, times *pi* equals 97.4090908 . . ."

I didn't even know what *pi* was!

Finally Norman descended the pole, rolled close to me, stood, launched himself fifteen feet into the air, and landed in his previous standing spot. "Hyper robot mode *fini*," he said, bowing graciously.

The crowd had gone silent, except for those who were madly running away. Fig and a guy wearing a headset were standing in front of Norman and me, their mouths hanging open like they'd just seen a walrus give birth to a monkey.

The man with the headset checked his watch. "We have to get this kid on the show, and quick," he said. "There are only eight minutes of program time left."

Fig, still looking goofy-eyed, simply nodded.

As Norman and I were being hustled toward the studio entrance by the headset guy, I looked back in the direction of my mom and dad. I couldn't see the Renault, or the silver car. I hoped, and prayed, that my parents were okay. *Please, God. Please.*

Then I remembered my uncle and cousin. The Rambeaus were under attack in two countries. What were our chances?

46.

Inside the building, Norman and I were whisked through a door with the words WAKE UP, AMERICA on it, and into a huge TV studio where we were guided past equipment and cameras and a boom mic, and by people manning those things, and then to a stage where we were sort of shoved into seats set next to each other. Dozens of bright lights shined down on us.

"Just do the same things you did outside," the guy with the headset said to Norman, "except for climbing—you'd be off camera." He retreated and glanced at a big digital clock, counting off time. "Ninety seconds," he said loudly to the crew.

And then a lady hurried up to Norman and me and patted our faces with a whitish powder that nearly made me sneeze. When she was gone, some guy scooted up and attached tiny microphones to our shirt collars. "Remember, the camera with the red light on is the live one," he said, before striding away.

It hit me that in a minute, or less, Norman and I

would be on national TV. Millions of viewers. Oh boy—
I really hadn't planned for that part. I was feeling kind
of tingly, kind of scared. What if I threw up? Or peed my
pants? I had to go to the bathroom for like an hour! Or
froze when the cameras clicked on? For the rest of my
life I'd be known as the Kid Who Freaked Out on the
Wake Up, America show.

But then I looked at Norman and calmed down a
smidgen. This was just something I had to do.

"Are you okay?" I asked Norman.

"I'm fine, Matt," he said, looking around the studio.
"But did I ever tell you that I consider television to be an
archaic medium? Give me quality French cinema any day."

Whatever!

Kent Cunningham approached and took a seat
close to us. Poop! I was hoping for Nancy, who's pretty
friendly, or even Fig, not Kent. He had gray hair held in
place by hair goo, but his face looked like he wasn't even
forty: Either his hair was lying or his face was lying. And
he was way too serious. And he smelled like guy perfume!

The mic guy slid up and attached a microphone to
Kent's shirt. "Twenty seconds," said the man with the
headset.

Eee-ah eee-ah eee-ah eee-ah eeeh-ah . . . Keep it together, Matt,
I told myself, wondering if I could even inhale or exhale.

"Ten seconds!"

Kent gave Norman and me the thumbs-up. "Let's

give the people what they want, gentlemen," he said. But I had no idea what that meant!

The headset guy put up a hand and said, "On five," then counted down with his fingers and thumb until they were folded into a fist. We were live!

"Welcome back," Kent said to a camera, in a voice deeper than it was ten seconds earlier. "I'm here with two brothers from New York City, Matthew and Norman Rambeau." He turned toward Norman and me. "Good morning, boys," he boomed, smiling.

Uh. Uh. *Answer!* I told myself. "Good morning," I said to Kent, weirdly wondering if my voice had sounded squeaky or girlish. Norman stayed quiet.

Kent gazed at the camera. "America, Matthew Rambeau is making a startling claim, that his brother is robotic, a machine. While this—"

"*Pardonnez-moi*," Norman said, "but I am NOT a robot. I am, in fact, an artificial, genetically enhanced, cybernetically integrated, bionically modified life-form." He grinned at a camera without a red light on. "Model number NRM 2000-B at your service."

"Thanks for the clarification," Kent said, throwing on such a tiny smile I wondered why he bothered. "Now, as a veteran newsman I am highly skeptical of such claims. But I have been told by Fig and by my director that Norman has some amazing skills. Robot or not, we may be looking at a child genius and a future Olympian."

But he is a robot, Kent, and to demonstrate . . . Wait, I was only saying those words inside my head. Ah!

Kent, eyebrow raised skeptically, gazed at my brother and me. "I hate to accuse people your age of fabrications, but when I look at Norman I see a boy just like any boy you might find anywhere in this great nation of ours. So where exactly is the robot?"

My turn to talk! "The robot stuff is on the inside, wires and hard drives, and that kind of junk," I told him, at the same time thinking, *Okay, okay, my voice* does *work and sounds pretty normal.* "But I can show you his power button and some ports. Or if you have a screwdriver—"

"Perhaps in a minute," Kent said. "But first I think our viewers would like to see some of Norman's impressive skills." He leaned toward Norman. "I heard that outside you were multiplying *pi* times *pi*. Can you do that again for us?"

Norman froze for a second, looked around in a daze, then started picking his nose. Was America seeing this? So you know, robots have no reason to pick their noses. They are booger free.

"Norman?" Kent pressed. "*Pi* times *pi*?"

"Sure thing, Dave," my brother said. Dave? Huh? Norman looked at the wrong camera and said, "Pie times pie equals cake. Cake times cake equals ice cream. Ice cream times ice cream equals—"

"Funny," Kent interrupted, not looking amused. "But seriously, if you could—"

That was when Norman slowly raised his arms like they were being pulled by strings, sneezed, and startled me by doing a sitting backflip. "Four score and seven rabbits ago," he said, "our crocodiles brought forth a new toadstool . . ."

That was not how the Gettysburg Address went!

Norman then wildly flopped around like he was sparking out, and threw himself onto Kent and went dead. Oh no. Something had gone majorly wrong with Norman!

Kent, his eyes gone wide, looked totally shocked. The studio was silent, like you could hear two ants talking, if

two ants were there and they knew how to talk. And then one of Norman's eyeballs, the one he had trouble with before, fell out and slowly rolled across the stage floor. The freakiest sound in the whole world? The sound of an eyeball rolling across a wooden floor. It was creeping me out!

"Holy Edward R. Murrow," Kent said, blinking repeatedly like he wanted to make sure his own eyes were okay. "I have no idea what just happened here." He looked down at dead Norman on his lap like he was wondering how he could ditch him.

Meanwhile, the guy with the headset waved frantically at Kent, then dragged a finger across his throat. Kent exhaled and peered into a camera. "Robotic boy or robotic bust?" he said in his smooth show-host voice. "We'll continue to keep a close *eye* on this story."

When the headset guy gave the all-clear signal, Kent peeled off Norman, stood, and handed the robot to me. "If you ever get this thing working right, give us a call." He turned and stomped offstage, toward a door that said EMPLOYEES ONLY on it. "I'm out of here!" he loudly announced.

I glanced at Norman, sitting in a lump on my lap and looking completely broken, and gave him a big, warm hug. But I didn't think he could feel it. "Sorry," I said to my brother, in case stress from this TV nonsense was what blew him out. He just sat there, broken. All

I wanted to do was save Norman by getting him away from the spies and on TV, so they wouldn't dare try to snatch him. This did *not* go as planned.

The makeup lady, looking kind of grossed out and kind of sympathetic at the same time, handed me Norman's runaway eyeball. I slipped it into the empty socket and gave it a twist, tightening it as best I could. Later on my dad . . .

My dad? My mom? Where on earth were they? I wondered. And my uncle and cousin, were they safe? Too many unanswered questions, as big as planets.

47.

A little bit later, Norman and I were sitting by ourselves on the twenty-sixth floor of the *Wake Up, America* show building, in a lobby area, though a security guard perched behind a big desk was keeping an eye on us. I really liked the view from up there, how all of New York City seemed to be stretched out before me. I know that most people think of New York as a crazy, dangerous place, but sometimes when I'm that high up and can see a big chunk of it, the buildings and traffic and bridges and the East River, it weirdly brings me some peace. I can't explain it.

Elsewhere, staffers from the show were trying to find my parents, calling police stations and hospitals. I had never been more worried in my life. I thought I'd be apart from my parents for ten minutes, tops. But it had been more than an hour.

And Norman . . .

I should have said that *I* was sitting in the lobby. Norman was stretched out across my lap, still fried. Looking at him, I felt totally helpless. If only I was a computer genius like my dad, I might have been able to figure out a way to get the robot running again. But I was just me.

Still, I kept trying to wake him up by saying "wake up" over and over again. Well, isn't that how you wake someone up?

"Wake up, Norman," I said for the seventy-third time. "This is a voice command override."

Nothing.

"Please, please, please wake up," I tried.

Nothing.

"If you wake up," I said, "I'll sing one of those Frenchy songs with you."

More nothing . . . Wait. Did Norman just twitch?

"Norman, can you hear me?" I bent close to his head. "If you can hear me, say something or do something. Give me a sign!"

Th-th-th-th-th, Norman snickered. Then he opened his

eyes, sat up, and gave me a mighty hug. I just stared at him, bug-eyed. At least I sure felt bug-eyed.

Norman was okay. He was okay!

"*Bonjour, mon frère,*" the robot said, leaning back and grinning. "So pleasant to see you again."

"Are you really okay?" I said, stunned. Imagine thinking your beloved pet hamster was dead, but just as you were planning the burial he jumped up and went for a run in his wheel. It was that kind of feeling.

"Tell me, Matt, did you enjoy my performance?" Norman asked.

"Your performance?" I said. "What do you mean 'performance'?" Norman just smiled. "Wait a minute! Are you saying that all the weird stuff you did on the show was a fake job? Just an act?"

"*Oui,*" Norman said, nodding. "While I have no formal training in the dramatic arts, I hope that my acting was suitable."

That was definitely the old Norman, the ham-headed showoff. He *was* back! "So why'd you fake being fried?" I asked.

"Simple," he said. "I thought that if I could show the spies and the rest of the world that I was junk, a malfunctioning 'robot,' perhaps they would leave us alone. And we could carry on with being just another American family."

Brilliant! Norman was brilliant! Then I thought

about what his words really meant. They meant that Norman's big goal was to just be part of a family. But . . . isn't that the exact thing most of us *people* want?

I was about to give Norman a high five, when I saw a worried look take over his face.

"Maman and Papa?" he said. "Is there any word of their whereabouts? And what about my dear uncle and cousin? Any news from France?"

"No news," I said, trying to sound confident. "But lots of people here and in France are looking for them. I'm sure they are all safe." I wished I was as certain as my words.

"Yes, they have to be okay," Norman said, blinking fast like he was trying to process something. He then smiled warmly at me, and I calmed down a little, felt reassured. No matter what was going on elsewhere in the world, I did have a brother, right there by my side. Sweet.

"You know something, Norman?" I said. "As far as brothers go, you're pretty much aces."

"*Merci,*" he said. "And this 'aces' is a good thing? Apologies, but no such word exists in my English language database, except as referring to a playing card, a person who excels at an activity such as an exam or a driving lesson, or a serve in tennis that cannot be returned."

"Yeah, it's a good thing," I said, starting to feel a little mushy. But since we were in public, I just punched

Norman on the arm, a little harder than I had planned. I hoped that I didn't dent the poor guy.

The robot and I peered out the big windows at our city. Far off, a helicopter moved across the blue sky. Closer, cars, taxis, and buses crawled along the streets. Millions of people were busy living their lives. Right there in front of us! *It's . . . it's . . .*

"Magnificent," Norman said, finishing my thought. I think I read somewhere that brothers could sometimes do that.

You know, I always sort of felt ripped off by Lucien's death, that life pretty much owed me a brother. But with Norman . . . Well, it was like the world was finally starting to make sense.

Just as I was about to go check with the security guard to see if there was any news about my parents, there was a sudden sound of a couple dozen shoes clomping up the hallway to the left of us. A stampede of people.

Then I saw them, my mom and dad being followed by Fig, Nancy, lots of staffers, and a guy holding a video camera.

Mom and Dad were safe! Yes!

Norman and I flew out of our chairs and ran up to them as they were hurrying to us. Collision! We all sort of melted into a big, messy clump of hugs, kisses, and tears. It was *so* good. So very, very good.

The show employees broke out in applause. I glanced

at the ones I could see, while clinging to my dad. Some of them, like Fig, had wet eyes, while others looked like they were trying hard to keep it together. Silly people. Go ahead and lose it!

"We're safe now," Dad informed Norman and me. "The spies are locked up in jail and aren't going anywhere."

Yes! Incredible! I hugged my dad even tighter.

"So, mister," Dad said to me. "I think someone has a whole lot of explaining to do."

But I only nodded and sniffled. I didn't want to talk—I just wanted to enjoy this moment with my family. I hoped it would last for at least a zillion years.

Norman and I switched, me hugging Mom and Norman kissing Dad. Mom smooched the top of my head, and then, I could hardly believe it, she smooched Norman's head. I heard Nancy say, "And so we have our happy ending." I was thinking those words were for me and my family, summarizing the crazy morning for us, but then I saw Nancy gazing into the video camera, and the camera guy giving her the thumbs-up. Jeez! These people.

The herd of humans we were stuck in slowly moved back up the hallway. Mom and Dad were safe, and Norman was okay too. I was the happiest kid in the universe!

48.

Downstairs, we were ushered through the doors and outside, where Dad's car was parked in front like we were royalty. I had never been so thrilled to see the old blue Renault. A crowd of at least one hundred people was gathered behind the barricades. Some of them were cheering and applauding, but others were taking pictures or saying not very nice things to Norman like, "Kiss me, R2D2!" I ignored them. I hoped Norman did too.

The security guard opened the car doors for us and we got in. Dad fired up the engine, we waved good-bye to Fig, Nancy, and the other show employees, and we took off. A police car then pulled behind us—our escort home, Dad said. Just hearing the word "home" activated my mushiness genes, big-time. We *were* going home. Yes!

By the time we were passing Zabar's again, this time in the opposite direction, I had gotten the whole scoop from Mom and Dad about what happened after Norman and I slipped out of the car.

My parents were about to run after us, when a traffic cop and a real cop showed up, eager to bust Mom for reckless driving. Mom and Dad explained in a rush of words that they were running from two men in the silver Audi a few cars back, who were trying to kidnap one of their sons. The cops looked skeptical, Dad said, especially since Norman and I had already fled. But since kidnapping is a very serious crime, they decided to check out the guys in the Audi. When they got close, the spies jumped out and ran. The cops ran after them and nabbed them a few blocks away. Yay!

Mom and Dad were taken to a police station, even though they were begging the officers to let them look for Norman and me. One of the cops said that several officers were already searching for us—mostly at TV and art studios in the area, based on what my parents had told them about where I'd said Norman and I were going—and that they needed to get a brief statement from my parents so they had enough to hold the suspects. The fact that one of the guys had a gun made their story much more believable, at least.

At the station, Dad was able to get the cops to contact Interpol, with hopes of tracking down Uncle Jean-Pierre and Jean-Pierre Jr. in France. But at that point there was no news, good or bad.

While my parents were waiting to talk to a detective, the craziest thing happened. Dad looked at a TV

and saw Norman and me on the *Wake Up, America* show. It was pretty much an *Oh my God, oh my God, oh my God, there they are!* moment for my parents, followed by lots of wondering about what the heck Norman and I were doing on TV.

"It was a surreal experience," Dad told Norman and me, his eyes a little misty. "I couldn't believe my own eyes, or for that matter everything that had happened this morning. It made no sense! And yet it made perfect sense! Logic coexisting with the illogical!"

Mom added, "I literally pinched myself to make sure I wasn't dreaming. Look at this bruise!" She held out her arm. "And then I was so relieved that you guys were safe. I began crying like a ninny."

"Ditto," Dad said, sniffling.

Hearing that, my own eyes teared up a little.

Dad then said that a small crowd had gathered around the police station TV, including the detective who was about to interview them. When Norman flopped around and his eyeball fell out and rolled away, the crowd went quiet, until the detective tapped Dad's shoulder.

"Those are your two sons?" he asked, and my dad nodded. "And one of them is a robot?" My dad nodded again. "Well, that's a little different," the cop said, scratching his scalp. "But hey, this is New York. I once had to arrest a gorilla."

While I was inside my head, imagining the scene at the police station, Dad glanced at me in the rearview mirror and said, "You've heard what happened with us. Now, without any further delays, I'd like to hear your story. You scared the daylights out of us. Spill it, cowboy!"

"Then I want to know what happened to poor Norman on the show," Mom added on.

I cleared my throat, hoping it would clear out some of the cobwebs in my brain.

"Well, you see," I said, kind of fast. "The Jumbotron in Times Square was showing the *Wake Up, America* show, and I had a sudden, gigantic idea. If I could get Norman on the show by saying he's the world's first robotic kid, the spies couldn't come near us. They wouldn't want their faces on TV, right?" I exhaled a gallon of air. "Norman and I were running down the sidewalk before I could think if it would even work. I just did it."

"And you did do it! You got him on the show!" Mom said, turning toward my father. "He really does have your brains."

"But he's got your nerves of steel," Dad said. "I'm going to start referring to my wife as Wonder Woman."

My mother rolled her eyes, but in a happy rolls-her-eyes way. "So they really believed that Norman was a robot?" she asked me.

I looked at my brother. We traded big smiles. "Only after I had Norman demonstrate some of his mad skills," I said.

Dad's eyes were on the road, but it also seemed like he was working on a thought. "Going public with news about Norman as a way to protect him . . . ," he said. "That's actually quite smart. It's one thing to steal secret technology, and a completely different thing to steal technology that has a public face, and a name. Millions of people now know what Norman looks like. You'd have to be an absolute fool to try and take him." He glanced at me in the rearview mirror and winked in his weird way. "Nice work, kiddo."

"Thanks," I said, feeling kind of smart, for a change.

I was expecting Mom or Dad to say that if I ever scared them like that again by jumping out of the car with Norman while we were stalled in traffic I was grounded for life. But that didn't happen. Instead, Mom peered back at Norman and said, "What about you? The police station was noisy so I couldn't quite hear you, but near the end of the interview you looked sort of . . . uh . . . um . . ."

"Like you had fried your motherboard," Dad said, throwing on a grin.

Norman improved his posture. "Papa and Maman, I will now tell you the story," he said. "I believed that I had figured out Matt's reason why he wanted to get me on television—to save me from the kidnappers—and then I had my own thought. If the kidnappers believed that my technology was inferior, they would have even less motivation to abduct me. So I pretended to be of low intelligence, and then I—" He glanced at me. "What is the proper phrase?"

"Spazzed out," I said.

"Correct," Norman said. "I spazzed out and shut myself down. My eyeball falling out was quite unintentional."

A few seconds passed, then Dad said, "Also brilliant, Norman. Who would want to steal junk technology?" He sneaked a quick look at Mom as we puttered up Columbus. "I think we have two brilliant sons on our hands, Connie."

"I have long suspected that was true," Mom said, smiling. And then the rest of us were smiling too.

My dad's cell phone rang while we were stopped at a traffic light a few blocks from home; I forgot to tell you that our phones were working again. "Hello?" he said. "Yes, it is he. . . . What? Are you absolutely sure? Great! Thanks so much for the news. But is . . . Oh, I see. . . ." His voice dropped down a rung. "We'll be home in ten minutes," he said to the caller. "Please call me there if you receive more information."

He hung up the phone and exhaled. The light turned green. We were slowly moving forward again.

"Great news," Dad said. "Jean-Pierre is safe. NYPD just received a call from the Prefecture of Police in Paris. No details yet, but I'm sure we'll know more soon."

"Thank God," Mom said.

I was also silently thanking God. But wait, what about . . .

Norman beat me to it. *"Pardonne-moi,"* he said, "but is Jean-Pierre Junior also safe?"

Dad scratched his nose. "Um, they didn't say anything about Jean-Pierre Junior, but it's early yet. We'll likely have more information later today."

I glanced at my dad. Even though I couldn't see his full face, I got the feeling he was holding something back. Could Jean-Pierre Jr. be injured? I wondered. Still kidnapped? Something worse?

Finally Dad pulled the car into the parking garage. The cop who was escorting us left with a honk of his car horn. Home, and safe. To be honest, I hadn't been sure I'd ever be able to say those words again. *Home. Safe.* Two of the best words ever invented.

49.

When we were inside our apartment, Mom hurried to her room, saying she wanted to change into fresh clothes, and Dad decided to scuttle Norman to the lab to tighten his eyeball and do a complete system check, "to be on the safe side."

All alone for a minute or two, I decided to indulge in the ultimate luxury: late morning cartoons on a school day.

As I was about to go turn on the TV, a big dose of woggliness hit me. Wow. Wow! I really did love my life, and my family, and our apartment. I wanted to kiss the walls! The floor! That Tiffany lamp over there! Everything!

And maybe I even loved Annie Bananas, in a way, since she was part of my life. And Jeter. And my school. And my teachers and Principal Jackson. Everyone I knew! And the spies . . . The dumb stupid idiot spies didn't ruin everything, didn't take all of this away from me. I was a *very* lucky kid.

*　　*　　*

While I was watching Nickelodeon and thinking about my morning—had I *really* been on national TV after running away from spies?—Dad returned, sorting through a stack of mail.

"How's Norman?" I asked.

"I think he's fine," he said, his eyes glued to the mail. "But the testing is going to take a little while longer yet."

"Any more news from France?" I wanted to know. "Did you try calling Uncle Jean-Pierre again?"

"As a matter of fact," Dad said, quickly glancing at me and then going back to the mail, "I was able to reach your uncle about five minutes ago." My gut tightened—he was being way too casual. Like . . . deliberately casual. "Jean-Pierre is perfectly fine, except for a scratch or two," he said. "We are going to talk more when he's finished giving his report to the police."

That was good about my uncle, but he still hadn't mentioned Jean-Pierre Jr. or the kidnappers. "So what happened with the kidnappers?" I asked. "And how is Jean-Pierre Junior doing?" The unasked question: *And why are you acting so weird?*

Dad set down the mail, hesitated for a moment, then came over and sat next to me on the couch. "Okay, here's the story," he said, running through the details so quickly I had to give him my full attention to keep up.

The details. The Jean-Pierres really had been kidnapped by the two men we saw in the video chat. And taken away at gunpoint! The getaway driver was my uncle's ex-girlfriend Véronique. Uncle Jean-Pierre said he didn't see her, but he recognized her "shrill" voice when she barked out commands to the two men. I wasn't exactly sure what *shrill* meant, but it didn't sound too pleasant. I'll always remember Véronique's voice as being deep and mysterious. *Sigh.*

Anyway, my uncle and cousin were riding in the back of a van, one of the men keeping his gun aimed at my uncle the entire time! Imagine how scary that must have been. Knowing that Jean-Pierre Jr.'s technology had fallen into the wrong hands, and certain he had no other option, my uncle said the fail-safe words. Jean-Pierre Jr. began erasing his files. And then he imploded!—destroying hard drives, files, circuit boards, and everything else that was keeping him . . . alive.

"It must have been just awful," Dad said, pulling me toward him. "Jean-Pierre Junior was as much a member of your uncle's family as Norman is ours. I can't imagine . . ." He swallowed hard and added, "Or I can imagine, which is even worse."

I set the remote down and tried to make sense of what I had just learned. I think a part of me didn't believe, wouldn't accept, that Jean-Pierre Jr. was dead. It was like I was expecting my dad's next words to be, "But then a miracle happened!"

Those weren't Dad's next words. He told me that the smoke and sparks from the imploding robot scared the heck out of them all. Véronique jammed on the brakes, giving my uncle a chance to grab what was left of Jean-Pierre Jr. and dive out of the van. He picked himself and the robot up, ran to the nearest house, and asked them to call the police. Last my uncle heard, the French police were on the trail of the kidnappers.

"That was how your uncle told the story, at any rate," Dad said, scratching his scalp. "But he always had a flair for the dramatic. It's possible that once his abductors realized that Jean-Pierre Junior's files and inner workings had been destroyed and he was of no use to them, they simply set your uncle and the robot to the curb."

I guess it didn't matter which version was true. "But Jean-Pierre Junior is dead," I said, my voice going all quavery again.

"'Dead' is not the most accurate word," Dad said, "but it covers it. Your uncle is going to immediately begin work on version 2.0, a new and improved Jean-Pierre Junior."

I was happy to hear that a replacement robot would soon be built, but would he be just like version 1.0, or a totally different kid? I was about to ask Dad that, when

Mom appeared wearing different clothes and giving us a quizzical look.

"Is everything okay?" she asked.

Dad and I weakly nodded, then Dad explained that he had been telling me the latest news about what happened with my uncle and cousin. "Not sure I'm ready for that story," Mom said, squishing up her face. "Maybe when my head is on straighter. This day has already had enough weirdness and emotion packed into it to cover a hundred days."

You know, I got what she was saying. I almost wished I hadn't asked my dad what was going on with Jean-Pierre Sr. and Jr., let the fact that the Rambeaus on this side of the Atlantic were safe and together be the only news for a little while yet. Does that sound cold?

Mom asked about Norman, so Dad told her he was in the lab, running tests. Mom said she'd be back in a minute, and left.

"Here's the thing, Matt," Dad said, clicking his teeth for unknown reasons. "If Norman asks about his cousin, maybe you should just say he's under repair. I know that he was fond of Jean-Pierre Junior; we all were. Plus, it might be strange for Norman, being the only functioning kid robot on the entire planet. Are you okay with that, shielding your brother from the truth for now?"

That made sense, so I nodded. "Jean-Pierre Junior is under repair" will be one of those lies you say because you care about the person and don't want to see them hurt. A lie due to love.

Dad and I went to check on Norman in the lab and found Mom there, chatting with the robot like they had always talked that way. First time I had seen it! "Just seeing how my mechanical kid is doing," Mom said, smiling.

Mom, Dad, Norman, and I then had this weird moment where we all sort of crazily grinned at each other. I think we were thinking the same thing, that this day could have turned out much worse for Norman and for all of us. But somehow we'd gotten through it, and there we were. Together.

"*Vive la famille Rambeau!*" Norman said, pounding a fist into the air.

Mom, Dad, and I said back, "*Vive la famille Rambeau!*" That means "Long live the Rambeau family." Yes, please. Long live us.

Mom kissed Dad and Norman and me on our heads, then left the lab so she could go phone her boss and let her know why she hadn't shown up for work. And then she was planning to call my school for the same reason.

"I think that Maman finally accepts me," Norman said, detaching himself from a HDMI cord. "As you Americans like to say, yoo-hoo!"

Cute.

But then Norman turned more serious. "Is there any word yet on Jean-Pierre Junior? Did he escape along with my uncle?" His eyes were big and wide.

I couldn't do it. I couldn't lie to Norman about his cousin, give him false hope that he would soon see him again on a video chat. But Dad must have been stronger than I was because he said, "I'm afraid your cousin was damaged during the kidnapping attempt, Norman. He'll be under repair for quite some time." He moved his eyes to the monitor, showing Norman's test results. All green bars, no red ones.

"*Bien,*" Norman said, looking sad. I wondered if he somehow knew that Jean-Pierre Jr. was gone.

50.

Hey, it's me again. Can I ask a small favor?

Now that the woggliness has worn off, I'd like to take back what I said about loving Annie Bananas. So can you please forget that I said those words? Thanks!

Boy, woggliness can sure mess with a kid's head. Loving Annie Bananas? What the heck was I thinking?

51.

Even though it was a crazy day, I was pretty sure I was going to fall asleep quickly that night. Norman was in his box, humming a French song.

"Matt?" he said, just as I was closing my eyes.

"Yes? What?"

"I . . . *une minute.*" The robot slipped out of his box, crawled onto my bed, and slid under the covers next to me. Even though there was plenty of room, it felt a little weird. I was used to sleeping alone.

"What about your box?" I asked.

"*Une boîte est juste un tas de bois.* A box is just a pile of wood," Norman said. "I would rather be over here with my brother. If it is okay with you."

"It's cool," I said. But if this started to become a regular thing, I'd probably ask Mom and Dad to buy a bed for Norman. A growing boy like me needs his space.

It got a little quiet, except for the distant sound of an airplane flying above the city. I always wonder where people are traveling to or returning from when I hear planes flying at night.

"Thank you for saving me, Matt," Norman said. "If Papa had said the fail-safe code, I would not be here. I owe you my life."

"You're welcome," I said. "Wait. I thought your hearing was off when Dad was talking about that stuff."

"*Oui,*" said Norman. "But recording was still operational. Don't tell Papa! My goal is to figure out how to disable the fail-safe programming without it being obvious. You do not get rid of Norman Rambeau that easily!"

Funny. And clever. The little rat found a way to hear, even with his ears turned off, and was now trying to keep from ever being imploded. Can't blame him for that. And I probably won't tell Dad. Unless it could lead to something bad happening, brothers are supposed to keep each other's secrets.

"I'm sad about Jean-Pierre Junior," Norman said.

"You know that he's . . . dead?" I asked.

"Correct. I sensed that something was wrong with Jean-Pierre Junior when we were in the car, like a communication link had been permanently broken," he said. "In response, my sensors tried to direct vapor beads to my eyes, but I am not built for tears."

It sounded like Norman and Jean-Pierre Jr. had some sort of connection that I'd probably never fully understand. "I'm sad too," I said. "But our uncle is going to build a new and improved Jean-Pierre Junior, version 2.0."

"I know," my brother said. "But I will always remember Jean-Pierre Junior 1.0. He was a *un enfant super*. A great kid."

Yep. My robot cousin was a pretty great kid.

"Good night, Matt," Norman said.

"*Bonne nuit*, Norman," I said, showing off some of the French I had learned.

Norman snuggled against me before putting himself in sleep mode, the power lights inside his eyes slowly blinking. I wish I had blinking power lights. That would be so cool.

Hmm. Maybe Norman sleeping in my bed instead of in his box wouldn't be too bad, I thought. At least I wouldn't feel lonely if I woke up in the middle of the night because of a scary nightmare.

Or because of screaming police or fire or ambulance sirens.

Or due to thunder and lightning flashes.

It can be tough when you're too old to go sleep in your parents' bed when you get scared or feel lonely at night, and too old for stuffed animals, but too young to be married and fall asleep with, *bleck*, a girl.

No wonder God invented brothers!

And then I slowly slipped into sleep mode, grateful for . . . everything.

*   *   *

When I woke up the next morning, Norman was back in his shipping box, peacefully sleeping. Baby steps, Mom would say.

EPILOGUE

Two weeks have passed, and the spies who were chasing us are still in jail on attempted kidnapping charges. All I know about them is that they are from France and were "vacationing" in New York City. Some vacation! One scary thing I saw on the news was that when police searched their car they found two handguns, rope and duct tape, a blueprint of Norman's design, and high-tech spy gear. Makes me wonder what they were willing to do to get Norman. And what they might have done to him had they been successful.

In France, the spies who kidnapped my uncle and cousin—Véronique and two men—were charged with kidnapping and espionage. Dad told me that none of the spies are talking to the police, but he's hoping that the truth will come out during their trials. Did they want to destroy the robots? Or steal the technology and make their own bots? It's quite possible, my dad thinks, that Véronique may have simply wanted to have possession of the robots so she could go public with the breakthrough and claim all the glory.

Even though Norman was a flop on *The Wake Up America Show*, reporters from all over the world have taken an interest in him, the world's first robot kid. But Mom and Dad aren't permitting interviews, and they even went to court to get an order from a judge saying that reporters aren't allowed within one hundred feet of Norman and me. But reporters are watching our building, and they shout questions from across the street whenever we are outside. It's beyond dumb. We are sort of like celebrities that the press will not leave alone.

My uncle Jean-Pierre is already working on the next Jean-Pierre Jr. Once the mainframe and protective shell are ready he'll start programming the robot, including Jean-Pierre Jr. 1.0's duplicate files, so we are all hoping he'll be a lot like the first one, even if he's new and improved. Jean-Pierre Jr. 2.0 should be ready around Christmas.

Some exciting news: Norman and I might get to meet Jean-Pierre Jr. 2.0 next summer. Mom and Dad have been talking about all of us vacationing for a week or two in France. Besides seeing the sights of Paris, Mom wants us to visit Lucien's cemetery and set flowers on his grave. She told Dad that she's finally ready to deal with Lucien's short life and his death.

The truth? Visiting Lucien's grave sounds creepy to me. I don't like being anywhere near cemeteries—also known as zombie hotels!—but I think it's something I should do so I can say hey to my lost brother. Norman feels the same way.

And even bigger news: My mom has given the okay for Norman to stay with us "indefinitely." That happened after Dad finally told her that he'd begun working on designs for an indestructible robot kid shortly after Lucien passed away. The conversation took place in their room, with the door closed, but Norman and I were sort of listening in, outside the door. I'd like to keep the details private, but I can say this: There were lots of mushy emotions going on, on both sides of that door.

This also means that no one has been talking about scrapping Norman after the year is out and building Norman 2.0, so I hope that doesn't happen. That would be weird, having to get used to an updated version of my brother every year or two. Plus, Norman 1.0 is already a big pest, as kid brothers go. What horrors could a new and improved Norman 2.0 bring?

On the other hand, I wouldn't want Norman to stay twelve forever. The kid, after all, wants to be a museum curator when he grows up. So I guess what I'm hoping for is that my dad and uncle figure out a way to gently let Norman 1.0 grow older and taller. It might be a silly wish, but if anyone can make that happen, it would be my dad and uncle. Besides, what's wrong with having a few silly wishes?

As you probably know, lots of scientists and inventors are racing to build their own robots. Not just kid robots, but also adult robots and animal robots, and I heard that some guy in Finland is working on robotic insects. Don't ask me why!

Meanwhile, my dad and uncle are planning to build more robots, for a totally cool reason. With Mom's help they are going to start a charity called Robot Friends, where robots will be given to sick kids so they always have a companion they can talk to and play with, even if they are in a hospital. I really like that idea. No one is sure what the world will be like when there are lots of robots running around, but I guess we'll find out soon enough. Me? I'm happy to be a real kid instead of something you can buy at Radio Shack.

One bad thing: Now that everyone knows that Norman is a robot, he's super popular at school again. But that's okay, because it's going to be a big day for me. Today is the deadline to sign up for the election to fill the empty seat on student council, and I'm nearly certain that I'm the only one who signed up. Soon I will be a government official! Who knows where this could lead? City council? The state senate? Someday I might even be the governor of New York. Hey, stop laughing, it could happen. All great leaders have to start somewhere.

Anyway, the final bell just rang, and I'm on my way to the office so Principal Jackson can tell me there's no need for an election since I'm the only candidate, and then appoint me to the vacant council seat. I'm planning to be a little choked up when he swears me in. Might say a few words.

I'm just about at the office when I see Annie Bananas, a thick stack of flyers cradled in her arm, tacking one up on a bulletin board. The flyer says, "Vote Norman Rambeau for Student Council. For a brave new tomorrow!"

Oh no. No!

"Hi, Matt," Annie says. "I talked Norman into signing up for the student council election. Won't that be fun, brother versus brother in a battle for the seat? Though I think Norman is going to kick your butt. And guess what? I'm his campaign manager!"

Grrr . . . Grrr . . . Grrr . . .

Now Annie is taping a different flyer to a wall that says, "Norman's promise: a new laptop for every student." Hmm. I guess that's a better platform than returning the soda machine to the cafeteria, or even starting a Stinky Sneaker Day, but no way can our school afford a laptop for every kid. They can't even keep the bathrooms filled with paper towels.

But maybe I better hire a campaign manager so I can come up with some bigger ideas, and cool posters. I wonder if Jeter would be up for it, though his campaign slogans would probably involve pirates. "Vote for Matthew Rambeau, mateys, or you'll catch the dreaded scurvy."

Actually, that's pretty good. What kid would want to catch scurvy? Maybe I should write it down so I don't forget.

While I'm hunting in my backpack for a pen, I hear a chant, "Norman . . . Norman . . . Norman," and see my brother on the shoulders of a big kid named Jason Reeves, surrounded by dozens of kids calling Norman's name. The computerized creep is already having his first campaign rally.

"*Bonjour*, Matt," Norman says, smiling and waving when he and his gang of supporters get closer. "Good luck with the election."

"Good luck to you, too, Norman," I say, waving back

to him and grinning. But this is what I'm thinking: *You are going down, robot brother!*

Well, friend, we are all caught up. As far as what will happen next with Mom, Dad, and Norman and me, who knows? A long stretch of normalcy might be nice. But I'm starting to think that the possibility of long stretches of normalcy kind of went flying out the window the day Norman showed up in his box. And that's okay with me.

Anyway, thanks so much for listening to my story, and for not jumping ship during the boring parts. This also means, you guessed it, it's finally later. High-five!